PRAISE

Sara Schaff is a graceful prose stylist, and her stories are smart and nuanced and rich with subtext. Connection in all its forms—the missed, the enduring, the complex—is the theme of this sharp and spirited collection.
—**Elizabeth McKenzie, author of** *The Portable Veblen*

I devoured Sara Schaff's *Say Something Nice About Me* over the course of one weekend. Schaff's stories come with a precision and momentum reminiscent of Maggie Nelson's *Bluets* and Katherine Heiny's *Single, Carefree, Mellow*. Page after page, sometimes by way of a trailer park tragedy, sometimes by way of a beach-condo vacation gone awry, Schaff delights and surprises her readers with universal insights by way of exquisite particulars. This is a gut-wrenching debut collection.
—**Hannah Pittard, author of** *Listen to Me* **and** *Reunion*

Here's a collection to decisively refute those who would dismiss "domestic fiction." These are stories of a devastated domesticity, of families and homes undermined by loss (of parents, of lovers, of jobs), and of their survivors clinging to one another. Schaff writes with great compassion and bracing honesty of the desperation of middle class lives suspended over the pit of poverty while taunting examples of affluence dance overhead. This is domestic fiction torn down, laid bare, stripped to the studs. These are stories about where we live now. —**Peter Ho Davies, author of** *The Welsh Girl*

SAY SOMETHING NICE ABOUT ME

Stories

SARA SCHAFF

Dearest Kathleen,

Thank you for wanting to read these old stories! More importantly, thank you for

being a mentor and an inspiration in those foundational days.

Much love,

Sara

Augury Books
New York, New York

Say Something Nice About Me
© 2016 Sara Schaff

ISBN-13: 978-0-9887355-8-3

Cover Design by Michael Miller

First Edition

AUTHOR'S NOTE

for Blossom Dain

How the wound of her new life healed.
How the heatshimmer shook
her vision afterward.

Benjamin Landry, from "H [Hydrogen]"

CONTENTS

Faces at the Window   13

When I Was Young and Swam to Cuba   27

That Won't Be Necessary   40

Ph.D.   58

The Condominium   71

Better Than Fine   87

Some of Us Can Leave   100

Say Something Nice About Me   106

Ports of Call   120

Shelter   132

Marie and Parker Threw a Party   148

Diatomaceous Earth   162

Acknowledgements   179

About the Author   183

FACES AT THE WINDOW

Our house was too big. It dwarfed me and my mother, who cried every year when we received the first winter heating bill. It left room for ghosts in every season.

But to the kids on my bus ride home, the house looked like a grand place with columns and porches and gray shutters on tall windows. It didn't matter that up close you could see the cracked paint. My schoolmates couldn't tell that the flat roof was covered in moss and leaky shingles. Inside we had water-stained ceilings and black mold in every closet. The rooms were wallpapered with peeling, hideous prints (lime-green bald eagles in my bedroom) and carpeted in stiff, brown rugs laid down in the 70s by the sister of the woman who had been my kindergarten teacher. The sister died alone, her naked body found decomposing in a waterless bath, a suicide. Soon after she was discovered, my mother got a deal on the house. We moved in just before I began the first grade, just the two of us. I did not know my father.

The house was surrounded by two acres of meadow, several of woods, and one of grass kept trim by a widowed dairy farmer who loved my mother even though she was unkind to him. We lived far from the small elementary school I attended, and I was always one of the last students off the bus in the afternoons. During the 45-minute ride along back roads—all we had in Helena were back roads—I stared out the window and waited. When I was in the fifth grade, I was teased almost daily by two girls, Angela and Tuesday.

"Rich girl," they would chant, their pretty mouths stained red from cherry lollipops. "Your parents have 100 cars."

Inseparable friends, Angela and Tuesday dressed alike: long dark-blonde hair in scrunchies at the tops of their heads, oversized sweatshirts that made them appear large and resilient, even though they were string beans underneath. I felt meek in the wrinkled button-downs my older cousins sent me from Elmira.

I should have known not to argue. "It's only me and my mother. And we just have one car." A Pontiac Sunbird with mustard-yellow, plastic seats. The car smelled like mothballs, and my mother had needed to borrow money from the dairy farmer to buy it.

"I bet you have 50 more in the garage."

"Or behind the house."

"Hidden in the woods."

When the bus finally stopped, Angela and Tuesday and the other remaining children would watch me cross the street. Sometimes I would turn around to see their faces pressed against the windows of the bus, licking the glass and laughing.

Once I was safely making my way up the long, uphill driveway, the bus would shudder and lurch on, and I would watch it go with some relief. I did not love my house, but I did not envy Angela and Tuesday theirs in the trailer park a mile away, where the homes were crowded into grassless, haphazard lots. The owner of the park tended the area only insofar as he threw gravel down on the main drive once every spring. In the winter, the drive went unplowed. One time I told my mother I'd heard some trailers had no reliable running water or electricity, and she shrugged. "That could be," she said, but she didn't look as aghast as I expected. It turned out she blamed the park for keeping the value of our property lower than she believed it should be. "I've put everything into this money pit," she said. "Don't you think some day I'd like to sell the fucking thing for a profit?"

People who met my mother often told me she was beautiful, and it made me swell with pride to hear others say it, though I didn't always see it myself. Even when she wore her wrinkled scrubs to the grocery store after work, men turned from rows of canned soup to look at her, but she never seemed to notice. She was too busy planning how to keep our house from complete disaster.

My mother had dreamed of being rich and comfortable, but as an undergraduate she fell in love with her married Spanish Literature professor, got pregnant with me, and had to drop out of college to work a series of jobs that disappointed her. According to her, my father said he supported her decision to have a child but not her wish that he be a part of my life. Instead, he gave my mother a small sum of money and asked her to go away. He would not let this mistake break up his family, he said. As I grew up and asked about him and whether there was ever a chance I could meet him or just see him from afar, she told me he had moved away, to some college town in the Midwest. She would not name the exact town or state, would only refer derisively to Ohio, Michigan, Iowa—places she had once driven through on a conflict-filled road trip with her parents and sisters. Her tone drew a picture for me of a kind of landlocked purgatory—a place with worse winters than ours.

My mother's family did not have money, but she had gleaned her desire for wealth and a big house from them all the same. They had lived in thrall of Aunt Evelyn, my great-great aunt and namesake, who had married a much older man, a former lumber baron from Maine.

My mother never called me Evelyn. Just Eve or Evie or

sometimes E. Sometimes nothing at all.

In her closet, she kept a box of crystals that had once dangled from Aunt Evelyn's dining room chandelier. She took these out at Christmas to hang on the tree in front of the colored lights, which she preferred to the plain white ones I asked for. Our tree always gleamed with tiny rainbows. When my mother wasn't looking, I would sometimes take down the crystals, and in front of a mirror, hold them up to my ears. I thought they would make lovely earrings, but they were actually quite heavy. We could only place them on the sturdiest tree branches—usually those toward the bottom or interior of the tree.

My mother worked late hours—first as a nursing student, then as an emergency room nurse—and before she left or when she came home, she'd take a bath and drift from room to room in her terrycloth robe, gazing from windows with her damp hair in a towel. She treated that bathrobe as if it were a silk dressing gown—hand wash only, line dry even in winter—though she'd bought it on clearance at Sears.

She loved meandering through the house; she said it made her feel like an aristocrat looking after her manor. Although she cursed the house for taking so much time and money that she didn't have, it did deliver tall ceilings and a grand staircase that swept upwards from the front entrance—double doors with intricate molding and the original hand-blown glass windows, which she said reminded her of the front doors of Aunt Evelyn's Queen Anne in Peekskill. On summer days, my mother liked to leave these doors open and sit outside in her bathrobe on the front porch to survey her land and the few cars that passed by on a road that was once paved with bricks. The house had a sense of history, which she said was important in a home.

She did not mind that a woman had died there. I once asked if she thought Mrs. Anderson's ghost lived in the house. My mother laughed. "If she does, she's got a lot of company." Our house was nearly 170 years old, built by one of the founding families of Helena. In a nearby cemetery, I had found ornamented headstones with their family name on it—de Groot. Many of the graves were small—little rows of graying molars—which my mother said were for the children who had died of cholera or scarlet fever.

Their lives had probably been both more opulent and more difficult than mine. Prettier clothes, shorter life spans. I used to worry that if I ever encountered one of them in my travels through the house, they would take one look at me and dislike what they saw.

One bitter February afternoon, Angela and Tuesday swept into my seat, shoving me against the window so the three of us were crammed in together. Angela sat on the outside. As if trying to block my escape, she pressed her hand against the seat in front of us. Her nails were painted a soft lavender, and where the polish had chipped away, I could see the dirt tucked underneath.

"You think you're too good for us," she said.

"You think you're better than everyone." Tuesday sat in the middle, jacketless, her arm pressed against the length of mine.

"I don't."

"Look at your stupid outfit," Angela said. "Your stupid face."

She had green eyes. Not long before, I'd run into her in the bathroom at school, just as she was fishing something out of her eye, rapidly blinking away tears. As I washed my hands in the sink next to hers, she'd said hello in a friendly, unembarrassed way that caught me off guard. When she'd traipsed out the door, waving good-bye, I'd felt lightheaded with pleasure and surprise.

Now I tried to imagine what she saw. I agreed that my outfit was stupid; I was tired of hand-me-downs. My coat was puffy, my jeans sat too high on my waist. But my face? I did not mind my freckles or pale skin. I liked how one of my cheeks dimpled, but not the other. I thought it might be a trait I shared with my father, although I'd never even seen a picture of him.

"What's wrong with my face?"

"Baby face," Tuesday said.

Angela nodded. "Because you're a spoiled baby."

I felt heat in my cheeks. A boy sitting in front of us turned around to peer over the top of his seat. "This should be good," he whispered to no one. His mother worked at the post office, where our mail was delivered.

I scowled at him and he grinned.

Angela and Tuesday chanted: "Rich girl, spoiled girl, baby face."

"At least it's not an ugly face."

Tuesday leaned close, her lollipop breath on my skin. "Ugly?" she said, mouth contorted.

I shook my head, ready to take it back, knowing it wasn't true.

Angela squeezed in further. I felt my chest compressing. "You think we're ugly?"

The words appeared to me, and I said them: "At least I don't live in a shithole."

They were quiet for a moment, and then Tuesday lashed out. Swiftly, with the palm of her hand, she smacked my head against the window. The crack rang out around the bus.

The boy in front of us gasped along with others I had not realized were watching. Angela watched me steadily. Her fingers tapped the plastic seat. Against my will, I started to cry.

Angela laughed first. The sound was bright and contagious, and everyone around us started laughing, too. "See what I mean? Baby, baby, baby."

As I climbed my driveway later, I felt furious at myself—for caring what Tuesday and Angela thought, for crying in front of them, for saying what I had and proving their point. It was the first time I'd ever sworn in front of someone. Shithole. I stood on our back porch and cursed the rotted steps. Some animal had crawled underneath them and died over the summer, and even through the chill in the air I could still smell it.

Inside, I could see my breath. I turned up the thermostat, then wrapped ice in a towel and held it to my head. I was alone as usual.

In my mother's absence, I wandered from dark room to dark room, lingering over the heating vents to warm my feet. I would let the hot air catch in my shirt, then walk to the vent in the next room. Some rooms did not have furniture. We could never fill the house with the few things we owned.

I stood over a vent in the upstairs hallway, gazed into one of the antique mirrors my mother had found at garage sales, and surveyed the gash administered on the bus. It was already red and hurt to touch. I kept touching it, replaying what I had said, what the girls had said, the moment Tuesday took hold of my head.

High above, the hallway light flickered and dimmed. A shadow passed behind me in the mirror, but when I turned, I saw nothing.

"Hello?"

Again, a flicker and a shadow. The de Groot children? Mrs. Anderson? I did not want to see the old woman. I imagined she would come in the form in which she had left the world, and the idea of her rotting skin terrified me. My own skin tingled. Behind my reflection, I could almost make out the shape of a child, braiding her hair. I tried to smile, but the girl did not seem to notice my overtures. She remained indistinct and disinterested, nodding her head to a melody only she could hear.

I made myself a bologna sandwich and ate it in front of the television. Every so often, I would look up, hoping to see the girl again, but she did not reappear. The house remained still. My skin no longer tingled, no lights flickered, no shadows crept. Before, I had been afraid of meeting a ghost while alone in the house. Now I understood that being alone was the thing that haunted me.

The next morning, an angry welt developed above my eye. It was a Saturday, and I heard my mother humming in the kitchen while I read on the living room couch. She approached me, carrying her coffee and a powdery donut. Her hair was long down her back, dark against her white bathrobe with its satin cuffs.

"What happened?" She touched the welt with her donut-eating hand, and I blinked away the powder that fell from it. Her touch was clinical and competent, as if she were inspecting a bruise on her own elbow or a wound on a patient's leg. I felt relieved to submit myself to her care, and I was nearly ready to tell her the story about Angela and Tuesday when she smiled mildly and sipped her coffee. "Another battle scar from recess?"

She could be forgiven for assuming; I'd been known to take a kickball or tetherball to the head. I shrugged because it took less energy to agree with my mother's view of the world. Also, I was still embarrassed by my weakness and my own, easy cruelty.

"You put ice on it?"

"Yes."

"Poor baby. Always had your father's coordination." She offered me the last half of her donut, which I accepted with an open palm. She bent down to inspect my hand.

"Filthy," she declared. "Make sure you wash under your fingernails, too." She took away the donut piece and dropped it in the trash.

When she left, I licked the powder off my fingers, very slowly, savoring my anger: my head was purple, and she wanted me to wash my hands!

My mother rarely spoke of my father, except at times like this—to blame him for our current woes or to attribute my flaws to him: my lack of coordination, my self-containment, my sizeable ears. In her blame, I now saw regret—what a life she could have had without clumsy me! And in this regret there was room to mold my family's history to my liking. Though I had never met my father, he felt as much a part of the house as the ghosts that belonged to its bricks and mortar and ugly rugs, and with his filmy presence surveying me, I decided that my mother was wrong: my father did want to know me, but it was she who had never let him see me. I suspected I had received other, more fruitful gifts from my father, and I wanted to uncover them.

A few weeks later, Tuesday climbed onto the bus alone, and I assumed Angela was sick or skipping school. She often bragged how her mother didn't care if she went to school or not, how she could stay home whenever she wanted. And yet as far as I could remember, she hadn't missed a day.

She did not appear the following day, or the day after that, and by the end of the week, I could hear everyone whispering on the bus: I heard Angela's name. In the afternoon, I chose a seat close to Tuesday's and leaned across the aisle to get her attention. She was staring out the window as we waited for all our fellow classmates and riders to come streaming out of the school and onto the bus.

"What happened to Angela? Where has she been?" I spoke nervously and kept my distance. Tuesday stared at me, annoyed.

"I don't know. With her father. Probably in Pennsylvania by now." She turned to the window, then after a pause, back to me. "Why do you care? She's not your friend."

I didn't answer because I knew the reason would sound unlikely—that I was drawn to Angela, even though she seemed to hate me.

My mother returned home while I was brushing my teeth, getting ready for bed.

She stood behind me as I finished flossing. Her skin looked flushed and blotchy in the bathroom mirror, her eyes baggy and tired.

Something about her face like this, drained of its usual beauty, made me want to confess everything to her—my loneliness, my hatred of our house, my longing to know my father in spite of what she'd said about him. Instead, I told her about Angela, how she usually rode my bus but suddenly didn't anymore, because she'd gone somewhere with her father.

My mother was quiet for a long time, and I couldn't tell if the reflection she was studying was mine or hers. When she finally spoke, she surprised me.

"When I'm gone, make sure all the doors are locked. Do you lock all the doors like I've told you?"

She had never told me to lock the doors, nor had she expressed concern about me being alone in the house. Her question now made me nervous. There were three entrances; I used the one key I had to let myself in through the back door. I never bothered checking on the security of the rest.

"And never let anyone inside, even someone you know."

"Did I do something wrong?"

My mother sighed and sat down on the closed lid of the toilet seat. And then she told me about what had happened to Angela. How she'd been home alone, watching her baby brother in the trailer park when her father showed up and kidnapped her. "But not the baby," my mother said. "The baby wasn't his."

By the time Angela's mother returned home from work, Angela and her father were long gone, and she found the baby shivering on a blanket on the bathroom floor, his diaper only half-changed. Angela's mother had rushed him to the hospital.

That was how my mother knew all this, because she was the attending nurse. The baby was still in the hospital for observation.

"I feel sick about it," my mother said.

She was watching me, and I couldn't figure out what she wanted me to say, though I was pretty sure she didn't want to hear I wondered what it would be like if my father showed up at the house one day, unannounced. Did he even know where we lived? Would I recognize him in some deep part of me, even though I had never seen him? I felt certain I would. While I sensed that there was something dark and terrifying about what had happened to Angela, my chest prickled with envy.

"How can a father kidnap his own child?" I said.

She misunderstood my question. "I know. Some people just shouldn't have children."

I woke at the sound of my mother's shrieks rising through the house. As I sat up in the dark, I became aware of an unfamiliar heat rippling beneath me. Quickly, I rushed from bed and ran downstairs to find my mother at the top of the basement steps, a tall, metal pot in her arms, water sloshing over the sides.

Seeing me, she cried out, "Call 911. The fucking furnace caught fire. And take Aunt Evelyn's crystals outside." She put the pot down on the ground long enough to whisk off her bathrobe and hand it to me. "This too. I don't want it to get burned."

Underneath, she was completely naked, and I looked away, but I did as I was told. I made the call. I grabbed the box of crystals from my mother's closet. I folded the bathrobe and carried it and the box onto the back porch. The robe already smelled of smoke and burnt polyester. I returned inside, filled up as many bowls as I could find, and carried them to the top of the steps for my mother.

"What are you doing?" she yelled when she saw me lining them up for her. "Stay outside!"

At the door, I turned around. There she was again in the kitchen, filling her pot with more water. Her skin was wet with sweat. She leaned over the faucet long enough to catch a drink in her mouth, then stumbled with the pot toward the open basement door.

Waiting for the fire department outside, I held the bathrobe and the box of crystals to my chest. I felt my nostrils freezing together and thought of Angela's mother discovering her baby boy alone on the floor, then driving to the hospital with his shivering body. I wondered if she kept him on her lap to warm him.

When the firemen arrived, they waved me over to their truck and instructed me to wait there. They said it wasn't serious, it wouldn't take long, everything was going to be fine. My naked mother met two men at the door. One was our car mechanic, and the other sometimes spent the night and made us scrambled eggs in the morning. I liked him; he was a good cook. I could hear both of them asking her gently to leave the house, but she just kept shaking her head. Now I think, what strange courage it must have taken her to stand in front of them, but then I just felt ashamed.

A few months passed, and the dogwoods in our yard started to bloom white flowers that looked like snow. Angela returned suddenly and without fanfare, just when we were starting to forget her. Her hair was chopped boyishly short, her lips pale and chapped. On the bus, she sat apart from all of us, even Tuesday. She stared out the window, listening to a new, purple Walkman the entire way to school and back home. Some kids said she'd gone all the way to North Carolina with her father. Some said they hadn't even left town.

I sat behind her one afternoon and touched her shoulder lightly. "Angela," I whispered. "I'm glad you're back."

She slid an earphone from one ear. She didn't speak or turn her head.

I fumbled for what I wanted to say. "You were right," I said. "I was a baby before."

She flashed her profile, paused. "Fuck off."

It wasn't like when Tuesday pushed my head into the window. I didn't cry. For a delirious moment, I even thought I could still win her over and convince her to talk to me. "I don't know my dad."

Slowly, Angela turned all the way around, and in her face I saw neither the disgust I feared nor the interest I hoped for. Her eyes were glassy and bored. A faded yellow bruise bloomed beneath the edge of her collar.

"Let me tell you something." Her voice came out flat and soft, and she almost smiled. I leaned closer, as if we were about to share a secret. "Your daddy doesn't want to know a dumb bitch like you."

She flipped her headphones back on. She never said another word to me.

I fell back in my seat, dizzy and sick to my stomach. I did feel dumb. Here I'd been inventing a kinship with Angela, when I didn't know anything for sure about her except where the bus picked her up every morning. Yet somehow she understood this one terrible thing about me, and as I replayed what she had said, it was not her voice in my head but my mother's.

Inside my house, I could finally wear a t-shirt and not feel chilled. While I ate dinner standing up in the kitchen, my gaze wandered over the water-stained walls, the food on my plate, the cabinets my mother had painted white but were now smudged with fingerprints. I thought of Angela's dull stare, her yellow bruise. I told myself I should feel lucky, but I didn't.

I washed my dishes, then went upstairs, where I searched her closet for letters, mementos, photographs—anything my mother might have saved from my father. I peered under her shoes—the high heels she never had any reason to wear—and ran my hand along the soft fabrics of summer dresses I'd only seen in photographs. I went through the pockets of her old coats and stood on a chair to search the top shelf. I found only Aunt Evelyn's old crystals, in the same inlaid-wooden box they'd always been in.

I removed two of the heaviest crystals and held them up to the lamp next to my mother's wrought-iron bed. I felt their cool, solid mass in my palms. Each one so carefully wrapped and cherished, while I could not find even a scrap of paper from my father.

As I held them, I saw my mother's bathrobe on the back of the door. Her silly, terrycloth bathrobe that she believed was so fine. From where I sat, I couldn't see the burn marks like spilled coffee on one sleeve. Like our house, I remember thinking—better from a distance.

Believing I would be relieved to get rid of it, I slipped the robe from its hook. For years the memory of this movement—my arm reaching up, gathering the cloth to my chest—would fill me with regret.

It was dark when I took the bathrobe and a flashlight into the woods. I did not feel afraid as I made my way along a path used mostly by deer. At the back of the cemetery, well away from the embellished stones of the de Groot family, a few thin graves lay flat to the ground, names of the deceased worn to indecipherable curves. I knelt down next to them. We were all quiet and unknowable here. A satisfying viciousness throbbed in my chest.

With just my fingers, I dug a shallow hole next to those stones. The vigorous digging tired me, and when I lifted the bathrobe, it felt bulky in my arms; the fabric, a little damp still from my mother's afternoon bath, had a solid, human weight to it that suddenly alarmed me. I laid it in the hole and patted clumps of damp earth around it.

Back at the house, I saw my mother had returned from work. I stood outside the kitchen window, watching her heat leftovers in the microwave. She still had on her scrubs, and I could tell she was looking at her reflection in the window, not at me outside, because she raised a hand to her hair and smiled.

This is still the image I see whenever I hear my mother's voice. Just one word on the phone, and I'm stumbling out of the woods again, the grass brushing my ankles. In my memory, the night is impossibly dark, and the kitchen is the only room that is lit. Framed in the window, my mother's smile fades, she remains very still. All around her is the house, like a vast and unsteerable ship. I take a clumsy step deeper into shadow, sure she has realized I'm spying and knows what I've done. But then I hear the little ding, and she opens the microwave door and removes a plate heaped with the chicken and pasta that two nights before I complained was too bland. In the sliver of light from inside, I can see my hands. They are covered in earth, and I wipe them back and forth on my jeans before I go inside.

WHEN I WAS YOUNG
AND SWAM TO CUBA

This was their first trip together as a family, and it wasn't going well for anyone except the newlyweds, who were all over each other like a couple of teenagers. This behavior baffled and embarrassed the four children, especially the actual teenagers: Marie's kids— Antonia (almost fifteen) and Jeremy (thirteen). Their mother looked so old to them! Dimpled thighs, frizzy gray hair, oversized, tie-dyed t-shirts. And of course they couldn't understand what she saw in Parker. He laughed at his own bad jokes but rarely smiled otherwise. His belly hung over the tight, jean shorts that he had worn every day since they'd left gray New York State for radiant Key West.

"I seriously want to die," Antonia said. She buried her head under a pillow to muffle the grunts and moans from the next room. "I'm suffocating myself right now; don't try to stop me."

"Please, let me help you." Jeremy sat up from his lumpy cot, reached across his sister's bed, and punched the pillow that covered her head. Her sheets felt damp from sweat and the humid, sea-salt air, but she clutched them to her as they tussled, sort of angry with each other, mostly hoping that by making noise they could stop Marie and Parker from having sex.

They only succeeded in waking the twins on the other side of the crowded room. Dara reached for Darlene's clammy hand, and Darlene sobbed quietly into her pillow. At age five, they didn't mind sharing a bed; they were used to sleeping close to each other, but they were not used to surly older siblings or a mother who always wanted to know if they were having a good time. They were not used to having a mother anymore.

"Is someone crying?" Antonia groaned. "Isn't this the greatest vacation ever?"

"Are you okay, Darlene?" Jeremy was only guessing which one it was. Darlene cried a lot. Dara never spoke and had stared out the window of the van the entire drive. When anyone said anything to her, she looked first at Darlene and then down at her hands.

"It's hot in here," Darlene sniffled.

The condo had problematic air conditioning. Also, the paint on the ceiling peeled from water damage, but a friend of a friend of Parker's owned the place, so they got a deal on the rent.

In the other room, the sex was still going on. Every night for the past three weeks, since Parker and his daughters had moved into Marie's house, Antonia had awoken at around 3:00 am to these grotesque animal sounds. It disgusted her to hear her mother like that. Antonia preferred her mother BP, Before Parker: a regular mom who made you dinner and listened to your problems and never displayed any obvious desire for anything or anyone.

"I'm out of here," she declared. "Who's coming with me?"

She threw the sheet off, revealing her thin tank top and her boyfriend's martini-glass-print boxer shorts. Her long legs glowed in the moonlight streaming through the sliding glass doors. Dara and Darlene sat up and looked over at her, both admiring and afraid. When Parker had explained to them that not only were they getting a new mother and a brother but also an older sister, they had imagined a kindly girl who would play school with them and French-braid their hair. Antonia, they seemed to realize now, was not this kind of sister.

"We can't go anywhere," Darlene said. "It's dark out."

Antonia was already opening the sliding doors, beaming with new purpose. "That's the best time to swim to Cuba," she said. Before, she'd fancied herself the persecuted revolutionary of her family. Now she believed she could get an army to do her bidding.

"You don't have your bathing suit," Dara whispered.

For a moment everyone stared at her. She looked down at her hands apologetically.

Antonia laughed. "At night you swim in your pajamas, silly. Grab your towels from the porch."

The girls sat on the edge of their bed, lifting their feet into the air and flexing their toes. "Don't we need shoes?" Darlene asked.

Jeremy pushed the twins out the door, forgetting to slide either the glass door or the screen behind them. "Let's go!" he said, spurred on by the force of his sister's enthusiasm. "We don't have all night."

Antonia marched toward the rickety gate, ignoring the condo's courtyard pool, which Marie and Parker had posed as a major selling point. The kids, of course, were trying hard to be unimpressed with anything that Marie and Parker wanted them to enjoy.

The condo was not actually on the beach; they had to cross over several sandy roads, all of them empty, before they heard the ocean. Dara and Darlene held hands, terrified but compelled to follow. Neither of them had seen the ocean before this morning, when they drove on US 1 from Key to Key to Key.

On the beach, Jeremy jogged to catch up with Antonia. The sand felt cool under his feet. "You're crazy," he said admiringly.

"Everyone put your towels here," she announced, pointing to an arbitrary spot near the water's edge. She dropped her own towel and started running toward the sea, her long hair fanning out behind her.

Even with the moonlight the ocean just looked blank, like outer space. Darlene started crying again, and Dara squeezed her hand, gently.

"Come on!" Antonia said. "You have to do it like this. You have to run in without thinking about all the creatures in the water waiting to eat you."

The twins had not even considered hungry sea creatures; the darkness was enough. Still, they shuddered and walked forward, holding hands until their toes touched wet sand. When the end of a wave swarmed around their feet, they screeched and ran back to Jeremy.

"It's okay, you don't have to go in." He put his hand on Darlene's back, and she and Dara looked at him gratefully. They were such skinny, funny-looking kids: their watery eyes too big for their faces, their curly hair in permanent tangles because they refused to be brushed. He couldn't believe that they were now, technically speaking, his family.

"Chickens!" Antonia cried. She dove into a wave and resurfaced, smiling.

"Don't swim too far," Jeremy yelled, surprised to hear himself sounding like their mother.

"I'll call you from Havana!"

"Whatever, Commie!"

"Viva Fidel!"

Jeremy looked at the twins, who stared morosely out to sea. "Want to look for shells?" he asked.

They nodded slowly, bewildered but pleased to have a task, and the three of them started picking up things that looked promising in the dim moonlight.

At some point, Antonia emerged from the ocean. "I almost made it," she said, panting. "But I knew you would all miss me too much."

"I think we could have done okay on our own," Jeremy teased. To let her know he was joking, he threw sand in her face, and they went at each other furiously, eventually involving Dara and Darlene, who laughed for maybe the first time since they had moved their bunk bed and Barbie suitcases into Marie's house.

When the sun started coming up, the four of them trudged back to the condo, slipping into bed before Marie and Parker woke.

"You could have drowned!" Marie shouted.

The family had assembled in the small, eat-in kitchen that could barely fit the six of them.

"A college student was raped on that beach last month," Parker said.

"Oh for Christ's sake," Antonia said. "No one was raped. No one drowned. Look! Happy as a clam."

She spun around to reveal her full health and happiness, and on her second spin, her back to her mother and Parker, she glared at Darlene and Dara. They looked away. One or both of them had told, even though nothing happened except that Darlene had stepped on a shell and cut her big toe, which she only realized in the morning, when she woke to find a little blood on her sheets.

Also, they had left pools of sand in their beds and on the tiled floor of the living room.

"We're sorry," Jeremy said. "We won't go to the beach at night again."

"Damn right, you won't," Parker said.

Marie leaned into him. "They're sorry." She was actually happy her kids had taken the little ones somewhere, without any prodding from the adults. "Let's have breakfast."

Parker kissed her neck as if he wanted to eat it.

"I'm not sorry!" Antonia screamed. "You're the ones who should be sorry!" She pushed past Parker, looming in the doorway, and let the screen door crash behind her.

"That kid has a lot of anger," Parker said. But he didn't want to criticize too much, not yet. It was too soon to be requiring that Marie discipline her children, who were, frankly, a little overindulged. "Ouch!" He swatted at his arm. "A mess of mosquitoes got in here last night. You kids make sure to shut the windows and doors."

Everyone nodded solemnly.

Marie started pouring pancake batter onto an electric griddle. She eyed the twins.

"I know you two love pancakes, don't you?"

Her voice was high-pitched, babyish, strange to Jeremy's ears.

"I'll make your pancakes in the shape of Mickey Mouse," she coaxed. The twins had wanted to stop at Disney World, but Parker had said it was too expensive and that the girls weren't tall enough yet to go on most of the rides.

"Thank you…Mom," Darlene said, watching Dara.

"Yes, thank you, Mom," Dara said, watching Darlene.

Marie teared up at the sound of these sad children claiming her as their mother. She'd been trying to get them to call her Mom since they moved in, but until now they had called her nothing.

Darlene had only wanted to say something that would make everyone stop being angry. She felt bad about getting Antonia in trouble, but her toe had hurt! There was a piece of shell stuck in there and her father was the one with the tweezers.

Dara felt uncomfortable calling Marie "Mom." Their own mother lived in Rhode Island now, and they weren't allowed to see her because she had a drinking problem and lived with a boyfriend who also had a drinking problem and had been in jail for hitting someone. Their father had explained that the man hadn't hit their mother, but another woman. They were very glad their mother had not been hurt, but they still wondered why she didn't come back to them or why their father didn't go to Rhode Island to get her. Was it so far? Only reachable by boat? They hadn't seen her in eight and a half months, and they worried about her almost constantly.

For a full day, no one was allowed to go to the beach. After breakfast, Marie and Parker sat by the pool and held hands between their lounge chairs. Dara and Darlene played Marco Polo in the shallow end while Antonia and Jeremy sat inside and watched television, bored and disgusted.

They had never seen their mother in a bikini before. She had definitely lost weight since starting her kickboxing classes at the gym, but they still didn't want to see her in the bikini, or Parker ogling her. They could hear her giggling, so they turned up the volume. It was a stupid morning talk show about how to style the perfect Easter look for the entire family, and Antonia wanted to watch it and Jeremy didn't, so they fought for the remote control, which felt better than their other options.

In the afternoon, they rented bikes and cycled around the island. This was supposed to be fun, but because there had been other restrictions to the day, the cycling felt like punishment to everyone except Marie and Parker, who rode a tandem bicycle and made a big show of singing "A Bicycle Built for Two" in harmony.

At Hemingway's House they discovered that Dara and Darlene were allergic to cats. Also, both girls were afraid of ghosts, and as they toured the grounds, Antonia made them believe that Papa's spirit watched them from the balcony of the house. They refused to go inside, and even though their eyes were itchy and watery, they sat on a bench near the pool and accepted six-toed cats into their laps.

Marie and Parker held hands and stole kisses during the tour, and Antonia made gagging sounds in response. Marie ignored her daughter, but Parker turned around, his neck red.

"Have some manners," he scolded.

"You're one to talk," she hissed.

Although Jeremy had questions for the tour guide—How much did Hemingway pay for the house? Did the son who lived in Montana get to come stay here for free? How much were all those first editions worth?—he allowed Antonia to drag him away from the group.

"Let's start our own tour," she said. "You're the expert, you be the guide."

In the writer's studio, he pointed at the typewriter in the

center of the room and made some announcements: "This is where the great writer penned such important novels as *For Whom the Bell Tolls* and *Death in the Afternoon* and the famous short stories 'The Short Happy Life of—'"

"You're going to be a famous writer one day," Antonia interrupted.

"Maybe." Jeremy shrugged. There were other things he liked besides writing: basketball and chemistry, for example. He also enjoyed birdwatching with their father. But he could see that Antonia was consumed again. He wouldn't get in the way of her ideas.

"When you're famous," she said, "you'll buy me a house like this in Havana. With tall windows to let in all the light, and in one room there will be a wall full of mirrors and a ballet bar." She did a few pliés and then an elegant arabesque to illustrate how she would use this future room. "You'll have your own studio of course, and you will visit whenever you need to break free of writer's block, and one of your most popular novels will be about a famous American dancer who moved to Cuba, became a principal ballerina in their National Ballet Company, and forgot how to speak English." She looked at Jeremy very seriously. "We will only be able to communicate in Spanish, dear brother. You'll pass along messages about my life to Mom, and you'll have to translate her Christmas cards for me. It will be a heartbreaking story."

They ate dinner at the Margaritaville Café. Marie winced at the music, but she kept a cheery face for Parker's sake. He was glowing. He owned all of Jimmy Buffet's albums, and in '94 he had followed the Fruitcakes tour around the country.

"A round of daiquiris for the table," he said to the waiter, making a bold and inclusive gesture with his arm. "Virgins for the children," he added.

Antonia and Jeremy snickered. Marie glared at them.

"What's a virgin?" Darlene asked.

Parker said, "It's a drink without any alcohol, Darlene, honey." While he spoke, he eyed Antonia, warning her.

The warning felt like a dare.

"Darlene, honey," she said, "a virgin is also a person who has not yet had sex, which is when, you know, a man puts his penis in a woman's vagina. All the noise we hear every night from the other room? That's sex." She waited for the uncomfortable silence to descend. "For your further information, three out of six people at this table are virgins."

As she expected, Marie and Parker gazed at her with horrified expressions.

Jeremy shook his head, wishing they were at home so that he could go into his room and shut the door.

Antonia remained nonchalant. "Don't worry, Mom, I know all about condoms."

"You are so grounded, young lady," Marie said.

"So ground me," Antonia said. "This trip couldn't get any worse."

"You need to start being nicer to your mother," Parker said. "Also, watch your mouth around the children."

Dara had never seen her father's face turn so red. He rarely got angry with her and her sister, although he always seemed very tired. She felt like she should be angry at Antonia for making her father mad, and for saying something that sounded inappropriate, but she couldn't stop staring at the older girl's very pretty blonde hair.

Antonia felt Dara's gaze on her and winked. She leaned across the table and whispered, "One day you'll learn how to piss off all the adults, too."

When the daiquiris came, the twins drank them quickly through curly straws. Without asking her father first, Dara told the waiter she'd like another.

Parker thought Antonia should not be able to leave the house for the remainder of the trip, but Marie argued him down to a lighter sentence: one more day of house arrest, followed by a month without phone or television privileges when they got home. The argument felt useless and ridiculous to Antonia. The punishments they were devising had nothing to do with her supposed crimes. If they didn't want her to talk about sex to the children, they should stop having it so often and so loudly! And if they wanted *her* to stop having sex, they could think again. Back home, she would still sneak out with Tommy at the end of the school day, before she caught the bus to dance class. He had a car and knew all the secluded spots in Milton Park.

In the middle of the night, Jeremy heard nothing from the room next door except for Parker's loud snores. Still, Antonia appeared restless, mumbling into her pillow and kicking at the sheets.

She didn't ask anyone to join her this time when she left the house. She walked to the beach again, but she didn't feel like swimming. Instead, she did a few handstands and then sat in the sand and buried her legs. "I'm the no-legged dancer," she said to no one. She made sweeping gestures with her arms. She sang a few bars of "Guantanamera": *Yo soy un hombre sincero...*

She felt very alone and melancholic, but it was a satisfying sort of melancholy, one that convinced her that she would do great things one day and make the people who had underestimated her wish they had treated her better when she was younger.

When Antonia returned to the condo, Dara was standing on the porch, looking over the railing at the pool. Worried that Antonia might have drowned in the ocean or been raped on the beach, she had waited out here since Antonia crept away.

"Why did you go to the beach again?" she asked. "You know you're not supposed to leave the house."

Antonia saw, for the first time, the girl's bony shoulders, the hollow, purple crescents under her eyes. "I've never heard you say so many words."

"I can talk fine."

"I'm sure you can."

"So why did you go?" Above the purple shadows, her eyes were shining now.

Antonia thought carefully. She wanted to create an air of mystery around herself; she could tell Dara was receptive to that sort of storytelling. "I had a secret mission. I can't tell you what it was."

"Please tell me."

"I really can't."

"Were you meeting your boyfriend to have sex?"

Antonia smiled. "I saw someone who wanted me to give you a very important message."

"What did he say?"

"*She* said to tell you not to worry. Everything's going to be okay."

"Was it my mother?"

Antonia had not been thinking of Dara's mother or of anyone in particular. "Yes," she said.

"She's okay?"

"She's fine." Antonia patted Dara's head. She was an okay kid, a little spacey. She and Jeremy would have to take it easier on the twins. They were just confused, a little worn out. She climbed into bed and fell into a deep sleep, sure that Dara would follow her back into the house eventually.

In the morning, everyone was in a panic by the time Antonia emerged from the bedroom. While Darlene sobbed, Marie spoke frantically into the phone, and Parker yelled obscenities. Jeremy stared at Antonia and mouthed, "What did you do?"

"I didn't do anything!" she said, and everyone stopped and turned to her. "What's going on?"

"When I woke up," Darlene said, "Dara was gone."

"I went looking for her outside," Jeremy said. "Where we were the other night? I didn't find her."

Before Parker could open his furious mouth, Antonia had bolted out the door and was running toward the beach.

Dara had been scared, but it felt important enough that she should go alone, without Darlene. She would talk to her sister about it later. After Antonia went inside, she retraced their steps from the other night. On the beach she looked both ways for anyone who looked like their mother. She heard laughing and far away music, but there were no people. She walked closer to the water, and then it occurred to her that maybe Antonia had seen her mother in Cuba, that maybe Antonia had made it all the way there, finally. She walked into the water. It was warm and impossible to see if there were fish underneath the black surface, nibbling at her toes.

She was up to her neck when the wave came, pushing her under. She felt the water going up her nose, she felt her nightgown bunching up over her head, her arms and legs scraped the ground. Time bent, time stopped. Dara knew she was going to drown and that her father and Marie would be angry at her for sneaking out in the middle of the night and drowning.

And then she was on the shore again, coughing out the water. In her confusion, she pushed herself away from the waves, crawling, crab-like. Her mother used to say that Dara and Darlene were her good-luck charms. Some luck! Alive, yes, but covered in sand and salty cuts that would sting later. She couldn't go back to the house like this. She would track sand and water everywhere, and then she would be grounded like Antonia.

She walked down the beach for a long time, stopping when she came to a plastic lounge chair that she thought would make a decent roof if it started to rain. She dug a shallow ditch for herself, climbed inside, then pulled the chair over it, over her head. In the morning she would figure out what to do next. She might have to walk around the island and find another family.

She woke when she heard people calling her name. Forgetting she might be in trouble, she pushed the chair-roof away and gazed around, blinking. Far off, she saw her father's lumbering body moving toward her. She saw Darlene in a sand cloud behind him, shrieking, "Don't be dead! Don't be dead!"

Antonia reached her first. "Oh, dear god," she cried. "I'm so sorry, Dara. I'm so sorry." The sunlight gleamed behind her golden hair, and her eyes were full, brimming over. Even her tears sparkled. Lifting Dara gently from the sand she said, "Don't listen to me ever again."

But Dara knew she would always listen to Antonia now. She clung to her tightly and closed her eyes. She couldn't remember if her mother's hair was dark or light.

THAT WON'T BE NECESSARY

Before the summer crew painted the dorms, they had to clean every room. In 303, Lucy stood on a ladder to scrape glow-in-the-dark pinup models from the ceiling.

Meanwhile, her painting partner was busy unfurling a stained, yellow bedsheet she'd pulled from a dresser drawer.

"Mind if I take this?" Steph cooed. "The thread count's incredible."

"Finders keepers," Lucy said, "words I like to live by."

Dirty linens aside, it was amazing the things students left behind. Mini refrigerators, toaster ovens, MP3 players, an almost brand-new laptop with sociology papers and photos of topless cheerleaders stored on the hard drive. That morning, Lucy had claimed a flat-screened television left in the closet of 303. She was simultaneously appalled and exhilarated by what her fellow undergraduates were willing to part with: appalled by the wastefulness, exhilarated by the hunt for new treasures.

Steph was singing now to the tune of "Uptown Girl": "One man's trash is this woman's new wardrobe…"

Lucy rolled her eyes; everyone already knew Steph's plan: to sew an entire line of fall dresses made out of the things she found in Jefferson Hall, the massive Pemberly Campus dormitory their crew had been charged with painting by the end of the summer.

"Cigarette break!" Steph called. With the sheet wrapped around her body, toga-style, she waved from the door.

It wasn't even break time, but Lucy felt relieved. Without Steph's background chatter, she could more easily daydream about seducing Gus, a polite townie on their crew. He had been her partner for a day when Steph was sick last week. They worked together on the second floor, where Lucy found the retro boombox, which she carried around the dorm with her, tuned to the local public radio station. Gus was a quiet guy, and she hadn't dared speak to him for fear of betraying her feelings. During the academic year, he cooked at the same dining hall where she fulfilled her work-study obligation by wiping tables and cleaning out the coffee filters between mealtimes. She liked that Gus wasn't a student; his life seemed important and real to her. He had a tattoo of a giant squid on one arm and orbiting planets on another. She believed that Gus was nothing like Patrick, the brawny and crass lacrosse player she'd had sex with months before on his narrow dormitory bed (elevated from the ground by concrete blocks) so that she wouldn't finish her first year of college a virgin.

By the time Steph returned, Lucy had finished scraping and begun pouring thick latex paint into her aluminum tray.

Steph laughed. "You're already covered!"

It was true: paint on her arm, her pants, her shoe. It took so little effort for Lucy to make a mess.

Humming a top forty tune, Steph arranged her drop cloth and painting paraphernalia with surprising precision. Even though she acted lazy and careless, she was—to Lucy's chagrin—efficient and clean when she finally decided to work. By the time lunch hour rolled around, she had completed her section of the room while Lucy was only halfway finished with one wall. Steph's purple bandana remained spotless while Lucy's dark hair was streaked with white.

She felt a painful jealousy flare up. She tried to fight off the feeling.

On her way to eat, Lucy stepped from Jefferson Hall into the bright sunlight, and Steph ran past her, toward her adoring crowd of male painters sprawled in the grass in front of the dorm. They laughed gleefully as she lifted her shirt to show an invisible dot of paint on her back. Lucy walked more slowly. She decided to hold onto her jealousy; it felt righteous, necessary, calming. And it made her feel superior, although she couldn't explain why.

Steph disappeared again as soon as Lucy sat down in the grass—close to Gus's shiny work boot, but not so close that it looked like she'd done so on purpose.

Paola, their supervisor, watched Steph go. "Doctor's appointment," she explained. "She'll be back tomorrow."

Everyone seemed to be eating sandwiches from the sub shop down the street, and Lucy eyed her soggy PB&J with regret.

"Probably went to the psychiatrist," Paola continued. "You college kids always want to talk to strangers about your problems." She narrowed her gaze on Lucy.

"I don't tell strangers my problems," Lucy said defensively.

"Not that you have any, honey," Paola said. "I mean, look at you." She grinned. "You're a mess."

This got a chuckle from the crew. Lucy was the one who tracked ghostly footprints in the halls at the end of the day. Out here with the others, she tried to laugh at herself, so Paola wouldn't think she was uptight. She liked to think of Paola as the mother hen of their crew, a skeptical delegator whose stamp of approval actually meant something. Broad and muscley, Paola worked for Plant Operations, tending the lawns and keeping dorm kitchens in working order during the academic year. Lucy felt that if there were only more people like her, the Stephs and Patricks of the world wouldn't get away with so much, and everything would run more smoothly. Unfortunately, and to Lucy's great surprise, Paola remained unimpressed with Lucy.

"I'm putting you with Carl for the afternoon," Paola said.

Carl smiled. "Best man for the job." The guys around him chuckled again.

Lucy glared. She got it of course: while some people could work alone, she was always paired with a more able painter. Since Tennessee Trent had quit the week before, making off with the laptop Steph found in a second floor triple, High School Josh had been painting the fifth floor on his own. He was fast, and as the only high school student on the team, he laughed at everyone's jokes too hard and never complained. Today Gus was teamed up with Dweeby Doug, the philosophy student who was only slightly more capable than Lucy: he painted slowly and never patched up the nail holes he found in the walls. Paola always preferred to work alone, because it was her only quiet time of the day.

On the first day of painting, just a week after graduation, after campus had emptied out and become weirdly quiet, Paola had explained that when she got home, her twins would be crawling all over her in their un-airconditioned apartment. "So don't act like babies," she'd said. "I'm not your RA. This isn't rocket science. Just do your work and don't bother me with your troubles, and we'll get through the summer just fine."

Lucy liked Carl only slightly more than she liked Steph. He was a tousle-haired and overconfident junior, another former prep school athlete like Patrick. She wondered what he was doing painting dorms. He rarely said anything about himself, but Lucy assumed he could be working in Daddy's law firm or interning on Wall Street.

Like the other boys, he was only too glad to bring Steph discarded garments for her future fashion show. Gus, on the other hand, barely seemed to notice Steph. During their lunch hours he seemed more interested in using the time for a little shut-eye in the sun, his sinewy arms tucked neatly beneath his head. Lucy believed that Gus would only fall for a more thoughtful girl, the type that was so quiet and watchful she made you wish you were inside her head.

At least Carl didn't talk her ear off. He finished painting a wall quickly, then went next door to start 304, a single. He was finished before Lucy had begun cleaning up her brushes, and he returned to help her.

"Slow and steady wins the race," he said.

He had an easy, genuine smile. She tried not to be won by it, but that's how they got you. And then they told everyone in their dorm about your over-eager blowjobs.

"I didn't know it was a race," Lucy said. Immediately, she regretted how surly she sounded. And then she regretted regretting her surliness. Didn't she have the right?

But Carl didn't seem to notice one way or the other. He stood close, holding his roller by his side.

"We do have a lot of rooms to get to by the end of July," he said. "If you're lucky, you'll be paired with me for the rest of the summer."

"If *you're* lucky," she countered.

She laughed quietly, not feeling like herself, but understanding that he was beating her at something—she just couldn't figure out at what.

He leaned toward her, and before she could retreat, he had pressed his thumb into her skin, where her neck met her collarbone.

She jerked away, even though his touch felt nicer than she'd expected.

"You have some paint on you, Lucy."

"I guess I get lost in the work."

"A true artist."

In spite of herself, she felt a little charming. She took a bow.

After cleaning their gear in the custodial room in the basement, Lucy remembered the television in the closet and realized she'd never be able to carry it home herself.

Carl agreed to help, and with the unwieldy flatscreen

between them, they walked slowly past the student hangouts that Lucy usually avoided—the coffee shops and bookstores and the curry-in-a-hurry joints—but which looked more inviting now that College Hill had emptied out.

Carl chatted easily, as if he were not gripping an awkward piece of furniture. His comfort made her nervous: should she have asked him to help after all? Did he think it was a ruse she'd come up with to get more time with him? Her arms were tired, and they had to put down the television for a moment in front of the Computer Science building.

She began to relax once she could see the dead-end of Main Street. On the quiet, tree-lined sidewalk, walking past the pretty colonial houses with perfect paintjobs, Lucy felt like she was in her city, finally. Reluctantly, she would move back into the dorms in September, because those were the rules—on campus until senior year—but for the summer she was subletting a one-bedroom on the second floor of a 1850s home, a stuffy walk-up with a stove in the middle of the living room.

Slowly and steadily, they carried the television up the rickety staircase at the back of the house.

"Here is fine," she said, gesturing with her chin to the hallway. The wide floorboards were painted green over a previous coat of lavender, which showed through in patches.

The television no longer between them, Carl back outside, he looked mildly nervous for the first time since she'd met him. "I have a confession," he said.

"You didn't help me with the television for purely altruistic reasons?"

He shrugged, a bit sheepish. "I first noticed you last semester, wiping down the tables in Woolsey Hall. You looked like you were thinking really important thoughts."

Because he was almost smirking when he said it, and because they were in an awkward arrangement—he with one foot outside and one still in her hallway, while she held the screen open, she didn't believe him entirely. She knew what he wanted, and she felt herself wanting it, too. But she was trying not to. Guys like Carl and Patrick were always looking out for the first-year girls. The ones who looked like they might never learn.

"I never noticed you before this summer," she said, honestly.

She pulled him inside, and when he leaned down to kiss her, she let him.

They ended up on the futon, and from there Lucy's eyes scanned the batik wall-hangings and sandalwood beads dangling from the broken ceiling fan. While Carl kissed her neck, she observed the corner cobwebs that she'd missed in the past. Everything here, even the soft sheets, belonged to someone else, the person who would return at the end of the summer. With all the windows open, Lucy could hear the television in her landlady's bedroom below. The woman was practically bedridden and watched the gambit of daytime soaps and salacious talk shows.

The sensations she was experiencing were pleasant, but her mind wanted to disagree, because this was Carl lifting her tank top over her head. This was Carl running his fingers over the flakey paint on her belly. She didn't want this, did she? She wanted Gus. A real man, someone who knew things beyond college, beyond entitlement. For all of Carl's confidence, he fumbled at her bra strap.

When it was over, he sat up and smoothed down his hair. "This was fun," he said. "We should do this again."

"Okay," Lucy said. She was already thinking about facing him tomorrow in the dorms, the snickers from the crew. She was already preparing to pretend nothing had happened.

To avoid an awkward parting, she climbed into the shower while Carl dressed. She expected him to be gone when she emerged but still gripped her towel around her protectively in case, and she was disappointed when she found her bedroom empty except for a lingering scent of latex paint and sweat.

No note, no request for her phone number. But what could she expect? Her mother always told her not to sleep with a boy after just one date, and this had been even less of a date than her first couple of outings with Patrick to the snack bar on central campus, where they had eaten bagels and pizza, not exactly candlelit dining. He hadn't even offered to pay with his meal card.

Sleeping with Patrick had seemed reasonable at the time. It was obvious he wanted to have sex from the way he came to her room late at night to sit on her bed with her, making her roommate uncomfortable enough to cover the mouthpiece of the phone and ask for some privacy. So they started spending more time in his room, listening to music and kissing on top of his sheets. Lucy did not love or even trust Patrick, but she didn't want to be a virgin anymore. It just seemed like one more thing to worry about. But even after he made it clear he was sleeping with other people, she kept responding to his telephone calls, she still climbed to the fifth floor every other evening and got into bed with him.

She didn't want to feel embarrassed anymore. This was her body. She should be able to direct it as she pleased.

Drinking gin she'd found in the freezer, Lucy wandered into the living room, with its high ceilings and the rotting floorboards in one corner. The television stood now on top of the coffee table, which Carl must have pushed against the wall while she showered. She saw that he had plugged it in for her, but she tried not to make anything of it. Sure, it was nice and unexpected, but Patrick had made a few sweet gestures, too: visited her in the library while she studied for finals, brought her chewing gum. Gum helped focus the mind, he said. But his mind had been on other things, especially in the basement of the library.

She watched a fuzzy episode of *Law & Order* and was so delighted by her first good television that she didn't notice how much she was drinking or that she hadn't actually eaten anything since lunch. She fell asleep on the couch and woke up starving, regretful, and late for work.

When she arrived at the dormitory, she found Paola in one of the triples on the third floor. Paola hated triples—"All that wall space." A triple meant more corners to clean, more potential for hidden and forgotten objects.

"Late, late, late," Paola said, eyes on her roller.

"Sorry, Paola," Lucy stammered. "I never—"

"Please, you think I haven't heard all the excuses in the book? I know this summer job is a joke to you kids."

"It's not a joke to me," Lucy said, even though on her walk up Main Street she'd been thinking of all the important things she wanted to do with her life—learn a dozen languages, search for long lost relatives in Belarus, join the Peace Corps, make a film— none of which included cleaning and painting college dormitories for a living.

Paola turned to look at Lucy. "Your BFF didn't want to paint alone today, so I put her with Gus."

Steph spending the day with Gus? Lucy's heart sank. "She's not my—"

"You want to help Carl with 307? Or you want a challenge—try 402 all by yourself?" Paola's expression was vaguely scoffing, and Lucy hoped she could make Paola change her mind about her.

Also, she did not want to see Carl just yet. "I'll take 402."

"That's my girl."

Lucy found the words mildly encouraging, but as she waited for Paola's expression to change, the older woman simply turned back to the work in front of her, the roller on the wall, white over layers of white.

402 was spotless, the way Lucy had left her dorm room after picking up the notebooks, empty lipstick tubes, and loose change that her roommate had left everywhere when her boyfriend came to collect her in his military-grade Hummer. Lucy wanted to thank the previous inhabitants of 402, whom she imagined to be small town girls like herself, probably in need of heavy financial aid, probably sexually inexperienced.

She would have felt happy about the privacy and the relatively easy room, but all morning she had to listen to Steph's high and nasally voice from down the hall. She heard laughter, some of it Gus's, and wished she were the one making him laugh. Hoping to avoid both of them and Carl, and still feeling guilty for arriving at work late, Lucy painted through the lunch hour. She had never painted faster, and by 2:00, all but a patch of one wall was complete.

Carl found her during their afternoon break. Blushing at the wall, she pretended she could not hear him over the radio.

"You want to catch a movie tomorrow night?"

The question honestly surprised her. She had figured he had come here to feel her up under her painting shirt. Or that he was here to tell her that he had been mistaken, that Steph was the real object of his affection, and he finally had the courage to really go for her. Patrick had actually said some shit like that, that Lucy was a "catalyst," that she'd "opened him to possibility"—his defense for screwing her roommate one evening when Lucy was at the library.

"I'm busy tomorrow."

"Hot date?"

"I have to…go to the grocery store? It takes a long time to walk there and back."

"I'll drive you. I have a car."

With leather interior and shiny hubcaps, no doubt. But really, he was making this hard for her. "Okay."

She thought he would leave then, but he hovered near her stepladder, and when she turned to him, she almost lost her balance. He rushed to steady her. "Thanks," she said. Still, he didn't go.

"I have something for you," he said, a little shyly.

Down the hall, she heard a yelp, a door slamming, the sound of rushing water in the hallway bathtub. Sometimes the crew rinsed their brushes in the dorm bathrooms, even though they weren't supposed to.

When Lucy was off the ladder, Carl took her hand and dropped something into it. She spread her fingers: a silver four-leaf clover, made for a charm bracelet.

"Isn't it a little premature to be buying me jewelry?"

In his blue eyes, she saw a momentary flinch, but then

he drew himself up, and the smooth veneer descended. "It's no big deal, Gus and Steph found it in the closet of the room they're painting today. They said it wasn't their style."

"And you know me well enough to know it's mine?"

"I just imagined that if you had jewelry, you'd prefer it simple. Pretty."

Why did she have to be so suspicious of generosity? She berated herself, then touched Carl's arm, and he pulled her to him for a kiss. When his hand slipped down the back of her pants, she stiffened and pushed him away. This was why she was so suspicious. "Thanks, Carl." She put the charm in her pocket and climbed back on the ladder.

Lucy finished 402, and Paola approved the work with a look of surprise—"No paint on the floor, good for you!"—then assigned her to 403, a single. All the debris in the room broke fire safety rules: scented candles, incense, an electric kettle, a hot plate, a pack of clove cigarettes. Too many hippies in college. It was a miracle the place hadn't burned down long ago.

She got started scraping off bits of scotch tape and poster putty by 3:30. And then time disappeared. She didn't realize how late it was until she noticed Gus observing her from the middle of the room with his arms crossed.

"Everyone's gone," he said. "Why are you still here, Lulu? You know we don't get overtime."

She flushed; no one had ever called her Lulu before.

"Why are *you* still here?" She tried sounding coy, but she just sounded demanding and accusatory. Gus grinned. He had paint near his mouth and on his right ear.

"Steph left all the cleaning for me to do." He shrugged. "I guess I pissed her off, so she's punishing me."

Did Gus look sad? Teasing? Was that distant gleam in his eye directed at the person Lucy thought least deserving of his admiration? Lucy thought of herself as a good reader of people, but she could not read Gus.

"Don't worry," she said. "She does that to everyone. I'm always cleaning up after her."

He laughed.

"What's funny?"

"It's just hard to imagine you cleaning up after someone, know what I mean?" He nodded sagely at her arms, which were patchy with white, but she felt that it might be an excuse to size her up.

She started gathering the drop cloth from the wall she had finished and began spreading it out along another wall to prepare for the next morning.

Gus bent to help her lay the cloth flat. She wouldn't mind if he pulled her close right now to inspect the paint on her, the splotches on her hipbone; even she didn't understand how those got there. When he offered to help her clean her brushes, she thanked him profusely.

He carried the paint tray into the bathroom, and she didn't bother telling him they should go to the custodial room in the basement. He smelled wonderful—of paint and vinaigrette.

Lucy blurted, "I always like your dinners best."

He glanced up from the tub, where he was rinsing her roller. "Pardon?"

She shook her head, feeling silly. "In the dining hall? When you make lasagna, it doesn't taste like mass-produced lasagna."

"My mother's recipe from the old country."

"Seriously?"

Gus laughed. "Nah. Just the way I like my lasagna." He grabbed the brush from her hand and ran it under the tap.

"You've cleaned enough, already," she said, even though she wanted him to stay. "You should go home."

He stood up from his crouching position. "And leave you all alone in this big, dark dormitory?"

With him towering over her, she felt her stomach wobble, but thinking of Carl's earlier earnestness gave her a spark of confidence. "Would you maybe want to catch a movie sometime?"

He looked embarrassed. "I don't think so, Lulu."

"I understand."

"Honestly, I'm flattered, it's just—"

"You don't date undergrads?"

"It's not that."

"What then?" She didn't know why she had to know, why he should even tell her, but she couldn't help herself. After everything with Patrick and her roommate and now with Paola hating her and this rash fling with Carl, she was pretty sure there was something wrong with her, something everyone else could see but her.

Gus closed his eyes for a moment and shook his head, confirming her suspicions that she was not as superior as she had wanted to believe. "It's just, my life's a little complicated right now."

"Oh, okay. Right."

"My son just turned two, and his mother—"

Lucy stopped listening. "I'm such an idiot."

"No way. Aren't all the students here geniuses?" He half-smiled.

"Obviously not." With her eyes, Lucy traced the rings of Saturn on Gus's bicep. Was Saturn a gas giant? She was terrible with facts. "I can get the rest. Really. I'll be fine."

She was afraid she might start crying in front of Gus, especially when he kissed the top of her head. "You're a good egg," he said.

She listened for his footsteps on the stairwell. Alone in the giant dormitory, the quiet of the building felt unnatural—gaping and cold. Thinking about it made her nervous, but instead of rushing her work, she took longer than usual washing the brushes, and when she returned them and her tray and the roller back to 403, she was reluctant to leave the room that had housed so many before her. In her brief experience, it was only the power-hungry RAs, the seniors unprepared for off-campus life, and the clinically depressed who got singles. Happy people did not want to live alone.

She lay down on the springy mattress and imagined the people who had cried, studied, and masturbated in that bed before her. The kids whose parents were forcing them to be engineers when all they wanted was to do improv comedy. The lonely Republican in a sea of staunch liberals. The hippy who'd lived there the previous semester and broke the fire codes. A California native. He'd probably needed the candles to banish the Seasonal Affective Disorder that plagued him since moving to gray New England. Now he was living in Brooklyn, starting law school in the fall and wearing pressed khakis instead of threadbare corduroys from the Salvation Army. If she saw him reading in a gothic library, under the comforting light of a banker's lamp, she believed she would observe the assured posture of a man who knew himself better. His prior sadness might not have disappeared entirely, but it would have dissipated once he left behind the things that had previously defined him.

Lucy sat up and looked around her, at the newly white walls, the ghosts of nail holes past. She felt calmer now than she'd felt since beginning college, which was funny, she thought, having just been rejected by the person she'd been fantasizing about for months. Already though, her conversation with Gus felt like it had happened years ago, and when her gaze fell on the trashbag in the corner, full of 403's debris, she thought, almost fondly, of the way Steph saw potential in otherwise undesirable discards. And she felt a new tenderness toward all the Jefferson Hall castoffs—the fancy cameras and used toothbrushes—things that had to be shed, Lucy decided, things that were no longer necessary.

The next day, Friday, Lucy was back at work with Steph, unusually quiet and dressed in a basketball jersey that High School Josh had found in a dormitory toilet, taken home to launder, and donated to her cause. Steph disappeared for a good portion of the morning to talk to Paola, but for the most part the two painted together harmoniously in the narrow single, and Lucy had to wonder if the shift in their dynamics had come from her or Steph. Looking at her newly quiet partner, she could no longer summon stabbing envy or indignation. When their backs touched by accident, Steph apologized politely but said nothing else until lunchtime, when the crew took their usual spots on the grass.

"I hate to leave you guys in the lurch," Steph said, "but I won't be coming back to work next week. Or any week after that."

Her imminent departure was greeted with a collective groan of disappointment from the boys.

Gus's reaction was almost imperceptible, but Lucy caught his sharp intake of breath.

"Family emergency," Steph said.

For a moment, Lucy's disdain returned: oh, the drama queen, the quitter. Poor Paola would have to find new workers or else poach them from another crew on campus. But Paola didn't cluck her tongue or roll her eyes. "You take care of yourself, kiddo," she said. She even stood up and hugged Steph in a motherly embrace, and Lucy had to admit that Steph seemed to be crying genuine tears on Paola's shoulder.

After work, Lucy showered and put on the dress she'd fallen asleep in the night before. She dangled Carl's four-leaf clover charm on a thin chain she found at the back of her dresser.

When Steph had said goodbye that afternoon, she had hugged Lucy tightly, as if they were friends. "Maybe you can be one of the models in my fall fashion show," she said. "After things settle down."

Lucy was surprised to hear herself asking, "Are you okay? Is there anything I can do?" She was even more surprised to realize she actually cared about the answer.

Steph shook her head. "I'm pregnant," she said. "My parents are going to kill me."

She hadn't said that Gus was the father. But by the end of the afternoon, that was the word in the empty dorms of Jefferson Hall. They'd been seeing each other for months, since before the semester ended.

In the custodial room, High School Josh swore that Gus would do the honorable thing and offer to marry Steph and help to raise the child.

Paola was washing her hands, and she had turned from the sink to get a better look at him. She seemed tired, Lucy thought, too tired to be annoyed. "Honey," she said kindly, "I sincerely doubt there's going to be a child."

When Lucy emerged from the bathroom, she was startled by the shadow at her screen door. She let out a tiny shriek.

"I'm here to take you grocery shopping?" Carl said. "I'm afraid you might die of scurvy."

She'd forgotten about his proposal to drive her to the store, and now his arrival came as some relief. This morning she'd eaten some yogurt that had gone off. It was embarrassing how easily she'd transformed into the helpless waif her mother had suspected she would.

On the sidewalk, she looked at his rusty, white Civic with some surprise.

"Sheila's my baby," he said. "I worked my ass off for her, and she runs like a dream, in spite of her age, so don't make fun of her."

"I wouldn't dare," she said. "But I did picture you driving something… fancier."

"Sorry, Princess."

It was undeniable: she felt happy! Embracing him with her entire body, she kissed him there, on the quiet street where mostly elderly people lived behind tightly drawn shades. "Instead of picking me up on a white horse or a Mercedes, you come for me in your rustbucket." She touched his shoulder, and then his face. "Don't be sorry."

At the store, they filled her cart with fruits and vegetables that she suspected would go bad before she could eat them all. They bought a whole chicken that neither of them knew how to cook. The next morning at work, they became permanent painting partners, and for the rest of the summer, they cleaned and refreshed doubles and triples with great efficiency—and occasionally made good use of the narrow mattresses at the end of the workday, when the rest of the painting crew had gone home. Lucy's former skepticism of Carl was replaced by a buoyant affection that surprised her, a feeling she hoped she could hold onto, whatever happened, wherever they moved on to from here.

At the end of the summer, Carl helped Lucy move into her new dorm room in Keeley Quad. It felt like a frat to her, so big and buzzing with kids in frayed baseball caps. She had wanted to live closer to central campus, but she'd had a low lottery number, and at least she would live in a single now. She realized she'd been wrong: happy people did sometimes live alone. She and Carl stood for a moment inside the new-old room, inspecting the paint job.

"The Keeley Crew had nothing on us," Carl said, pointing at some leftover poster putty.

"Those Jefferson kids don't know how lucky they are," Lucy said. They made her narrow bed and got into it.

"How many have fucked here before us?" Lucy wondered.

"How many Pulitzer Prize winners?"

"How many philandering politicians?"

They could hear muffled voices next door and someone pounding nails into the wall.

Gracefully, Carl unhooked her bra. He'd learned a lot over the summer.

Later, they walked around campus, gazing at the new students, stumbling around with their parents and armloads of stuff for their rooms: egg crates for their meager mattresses, plush comforters, bulletin boards to post photos of their friends from home. On Goode Street, they found a stocky girl whose shoulders sagged from the plastic bags she carried uphill, from the mall downtown. Her mother and father called to her from a block behind, struggling to catch up, but she didn't turn around or stop for them; she just barreled forward, toward Pemberly Campus, and Lucy and Carl stayed close behind, claiming her as their own.

"She's grown up so fast," Lucy whispered. "*Too* fast."

"I hate to leave her," Carl said. "Our lives will feel so empty."

"At least I still have my book club."

"And I have Simon."

"Who's Simon?"

"My private Pilates instructor."

"Yes, thank God for Simon."

They laughed in a showy manner that suited their playacting, but when Lucy glanced again at Carl, she felt fluttery and vulnerable, as if she were losing something real.

PH.D.

In reality they all lived in a kind of hieroglyphic world,
where the real thing was never said or done or even thought,
but only represented by a set of arbitrary signs.

Edith Wharton, *The Age of Innocence*

Research

Thinking I might run into you at the library today, I stopped by
your carrel. Empty except for a few, slim volumes. Don't you have
a dissertation to finish? I thought of your fantasy: the cool cement
walls, the occasional click of heels in the stacks. If you had come by,
I would have lifted my skirt.

But you didn't come by, and I walked downtown feeling
exposed. The weather was good, so I thought I might see you

strolling in your t-shirt and shorts. I wandered through the farmers'
market, bought five Brandy Wine tomatoes from that Amish
beauty. She wore our favorite blue dress, surprisingly flattering for
its prairie shape. Her blonde curls poked beneath the edges of her
cap. *One hot bonnet*, you said when we spotted her last summer. I
laughed: our little Amish joke.

Today in the crowd of people trawling for local produce,
I saw a man who looked like you from a distance. He called to a
woman buying peaches, very pregnant, carrying a basket of carrots,
collards, and sunflowers. It's the kind of scene you would have
made fun of—*self-satisfied, future baby-sling-wearing, hybrid-driving
liberals*. And yet in teasing you would have revealed both how much
you actually wanted that life and how you were not entirely sure
you wanted it with me.

Knowing I shouldn't, I left the tomatoes on your porch
swing. Your car was not in the driveway, and I walked home in a
fluster, berating myself for being silly enough to want to buy you
locally grown produce.

I returned hours later, concerned that an unmarked bag
of tomatoes might look suspicious—or worse, like trash. The
idea was to take them home with me, turn them into something
useful, like a sane, summery salad with basil and mozzarella.
The bag of tomatoes had disappeared. I saw a light in your office
window, which got my hopes up, but it was only the glow from
your screensaver. I looked for shadows. I listened for voices coming
through an open window. I felt ill as I watched from behind a tree.

But I did not move until a dog-walker stopped nearby, then
squatted to retrieve her poodle's tiny shit. A demeaning task, we
agreed once, when we considered rescuing a greyhound together.
And how embarrassing for the dog—no privacy! This woman did
not even look away, but congratulated her pooch on its instinctive
behavior. I'm quite glad we decided not to adopt. Who would walk
the dog now? Who would feed it?

Standing in front of your apartment, I half-expected to see
you traipsing home with Miriam. Before you moved out last month,

you said you were ambivalent about her advances. She makes you crazy because she believes in the superiority of archaeology— (tangible objects!)—over your great passion, Medieval French poetry (so subjective and, frankly, a little too obsessed with martyrs and saints). Here is what I imagine: she has been calling you in the middle of the night from the Ancient Roman wing of the museum. Right now, she's probably giving you a private and illuminating tour of Etruscan vases. Miriam could be beautiful, but she refuses to moisturize and has poor fashion sense: saggy overalls and threadbare t-shirts. A person would never be able to make her see the benefits of a flattering wrap dress. Rumors in the Comp Lit and English crowd suggest that you have admitted she looks good naked, in spite of all the body hair.

I find Miriam's lack of vanity almost grotesque. But if I had met her separately from you, I imagine I might have liked her.

Preliminary Exams

I read for days without stopping to eat: *EliotHardyJamesBrontesWoolfAustenDickens.* We hadn't been dating long, and you stopped by my apartment when I didn't return your calls. You took one look at my gray skin and went right out the door for takeout, returning with chicken shawarma and lots of napkins, because you knew I would make a ravenous mess. You placed my foil-wrapped sandwich in my open palm, very gently.

"This will put the color back in your cheeks," you said. Lifting a sliver of meat from the sandwich, you fed it to me as delicately as a mother bird.

Then you cast an eye over the storm of papers and open texts on the living room floor. "Remember," you said, "you're not inventing the atomic bomb here." You turned on the TV and we watched hours of home improvement programming.

When I was down to a few hours before the exam, I resorted to Sparknotes. I'm embarrassed to admit it, but in my defense, it was all to fill in gaps in plot. I knew all there was to know about the characters and their motivations.

Title Page: Untitled
(OR *Each Time You Happen to Me All Over Again*)

Chapters 1-2: Obsession, the Better Self, and the Seven-Year Itch

To get your PhD in the humanities, you need an obsessive nature. One might even say the process of writing a dissertation requires the sensibility of a stalker. Why else would we all be working for so long on one topic when the chance of us getting tenure-track appointments is about as likely as getting discovered by a Hollywood scout in the food court at the mall?

A long time ago, I wanted to be an expert. In the third grade I had an accomplished imaginary friend called Marietta Divina. She sang opera all over the world, wrote bestselling novels, and dreamed of being awarded the Nobel Peace Prize before she turned twenty. In January of that year, just as my parents were divorcing, Marietta announced her intention to go back to school to get her PhD in anthropology. I never saw her again but received letters from her in which she detailed her research in an undiscovered Amazon village. She'd fallen in love with the chief, would soon become a princess, and was being hailed by the villagers for her crystalline voice and for her facility with their complex language, which contained over one hundred words for the verb "to do."

I decided to be *that* kind of doctor.

Nineteen years later when I started grad school, I thought I would enjoy stalking Edith Wharton around the globe. She reminded me of Marietta: born into privilege, financially independent enough to write and travel. I feel a kinship with her that I've never felt with another modern writer. Her characters are complicated—worldly yet confused, calculating but unhappy, well-intentioned but often ruined. Recently discovered letters to Wharton's childhood German governess profess effusive gratefulness and loyalty. But in her autobiography the governess is barely a footnote.

At the beginning of the summer, when things were already going badly between us, I made the trip alone to The Mount to see the beautiful grounds. It made me very sad to see the run-down state of things and not be able to complain about it to anyone but the docents.

One of my advisors calls Edith the Jackie Collins of early 20th century American Literature. He does not mean this in a good way, of course, but I'm interested in the idea of a self re-made for another time. Probably because I have to admit that watching for you, while good for an initial adrenaline rush, has become tiresome and isolating. I've started having dreams about trysts with Henry James and Graham Greene. I picture myself driving around old Havana in a '54 Chevy with Hemingway.

In one persistent fantasy, I'm snowed in at a New England bed and breakfast, and who serves me my eggs Benedict but John Fucking Updike. He allows me just one bite before he pulls me from my captain's chair, leads me through the swinging door to the kitchen—all the guests at the dining table stare in shock—and screws me in the pantry, where I manage to pull down an entire shelf of beautifully canned peaches. As I pull up my stockings afterwards, John smoothes his red-striped apron. I suggest another round, but he's already putting together a tray of tea and biscuits for the couple in the Maple room; they have requested room service. "The roads should be plowed by now," he says. "You'll be able to make check-out time."

Chapters 3-4: When Nothing Adds Up, or When Everything Does

I admit that I checked the garbage cans and the compost in back of your apartment. I can see how bringing a flashlight for the task might look like premeditation, the work of a mind unhinged. I saw tomatoes on the top of the heap, but they looked too old to be the fresh heirlooms I had bought for you. As I caught myself reaching into the compost barrel, fingertips almost touching wrinkled, organic matter covered in coffee grounds, I drew back in horror at what I'd become. I resolved to engage in healthier leisure activities.

I trudged home and lay on my living room floor. Even when it gets hot outside, the hardwood remains cool. The last time I saw you—just last week, isn't that a kick!—we spent some time there. You lifted my dress with one hand as your other hand pushed my shoulder into the floorboards. It was a sharp, not unpleasant feeling. You had been so distant since our breakup, but here you were; my discomfort proved it. The front door was open, the screen door latched, and I heard the mailman's familiar shuffle on the porch, just before you finished.

And then you left so abruptly, mumbling about *being out of touch.*

You could have been more specific, that would have been useful.

And I could have been more direct: *Tell me what the hell is going on: Will you be out of touch while fucking Miriam? Does she honestly look good naked?*

And yet, I nodded you away without a *why?* or a *what?* It's been a genuinely difficult year for you. Your father has been ill, and you've considered taking off some time to be with him in Maine. Your advisor is having a fit, concerned you'll become a doctoral casualty, just another ABD. But he shouldn't worry; you're dedicated to completing (almost) everything you start.

You might even be back with your family now, too busy to remember me. And if you are home, you might see Carla, the high school sweetheart who haunts your dreams, wearing the sundress she had on the night you broke up with her. She recently found you on a popular social networking site that we all visit more than the library. Because she refuses to post a picture of herself, I still have no idea what she looks like. I have imagined the Buttercupbeauty you remember from childhood, but I suspect she has aged terribly—as women who never leave their hometowns tend to do—and this will grieve you. You could be at the pharmacy on old Main Street, picking up a prescription for your father, and she appears right in front of you, pushing a baby in a stroller, pulling a squirmy toddler by the wrist. *Unrecognizable*, you will say later about her puffy face. And yet you want to lean her against the shelves of band-aids. You would do it, too, except her husband shows up, a guy you used to drink with in high school.

Determined not to wallow in self-pity all night, I headed to the refrigerator for ingredients. I moved all the eggplants to the counter, where I sliced them with vicious precision. Roasted eggplant is not your favorite dish. I make it when I'm alone. Searching through the refrigerator for feta, I had to move aside almost-empty bottles of ketchup, hot sauce, and mustard. For some reason, each half-consumed condiment reminded me of you. Remember when you suggested I give up academia and write a cookbook? I should have been pissed, but you complemented my pork pozole, smoothed my hair back, and kissed my neck. You made me a midnight espresso, dark and creamy. Afterward, we watched late night television until it was early. You always know how to ploy me: with sex, caffeine, and a live studio audience.

Remember how just before we started dating, you hooked up with Rebecca, the raven-haired Norwegian-Uruguayan Comp Lit. student who dropped out to live with a Microsoft exec? You thought you were destined to marry her because she has the same last name, only spelled differently. Also, she looked a little like Carrie Fisher in her Princess Leia years. But she ran away, you mourned, and I got drunk at Zander's Halloween party. That was the first year, and apparently I didn't get the sexy memo; I came dressed as the Cowardly Lion. I had spent hours papier mâché-ing the head and painting it. But I took inaccurate measurements and the too-small mask made my face sweat. I had pinned the tail of yarn to my savannah-colored corduroys from the Salvation Army. You tugged on it to get my attention, and when you pulled the mask from my head, I could see my face reflected in your dark eyes: shiny with sweat.

You debuted the Naked Chef that year. And now a Halloween party isn't complete unless you show up shirtless, in your apron and boxers. The irony is that you're a terrible cook. I never could say it to your face before, but it feels like the right time to tell you how much I always hated your overstuffed breakfast burritos.

Back then you had me fooled with the banana crepes you were passing out on compostable plates. (I found out later that your roommate had actually made the light and airy pancakes.) Also, I was lonely. I hate the Midwest. It's windy here and there are no hills, and as a pedestrian, I fear for my life; no one pays attention to traffic laws and everyone drives enormous cars.

Without you here to talk to, I have time to think about everything in frustrating detail. I should thank you for disappearing. For not answering your emails. For not returning my calls.

Of course, you might be at your father's funeral, weeping into your dear mother's shoulder.

Or, *you* might be dead, your face pressed against the windshield of Miriam's or Carla's car, the hood of the car crumpled up against a tree.

While chopping garlic, I sliced my finger. Holding it above my head, pressed into a dirty dishtowel, I could not stop laughing. If you were here, you would have been running around, getting the hydrogen peroxide and sterile bandages. You can be thoughtful like that. You worry about germs.

Footnote: One Man's Thesis is Another Man's Sore Spot

I never explained my theory about grad school. It's just like high school, but with more complicated words to describe the same emotional bullshit. I'm in the marching band, and you're in the popular crowd. Girls like you because you take your shirt off for

Halloween and perform higher-education themed lyrics to popular songs—*All the literate ladies! All the literate ladies!*

At the end of the spring semester, we hosted what would be our last barbeque together. While talking to a group of first-years in Women's Studies, I pointed to you across the lawn. You were playing cornhole, a game I will never understand the charm of, and one of these women looked at me jealously and called you a "humanities hottie."

When I told you later about your new fan and the title she'd bestowed on you, you were offended—not because she had objectified you but because she'd qualified your hotness. When I chuckled at your annoyance, you snapped, "It's not actually that funny."

I guess I should have realized it sooner: you have a sense of humor about everything but yourself.

Annotated Bibliography

Wharton, Edith. *Custom of the Country.*

It's easy to loathe Undine Spragg, Wharton's vain and beautiful social-climber. She advances through society and husbands by a process of imitation, not understanding. Her third husband, the French aristocrat Raymond de Chelles, is at first charmed, then finally horrified, by her designs: "You come among us speaking our language and not knowing what we mean; wanting the things we want, and not knowing why we want them; aping our weaknesses, exaggerating our follies, ignoring or ridiculing all we care about." (334)

I'm tired of people clamoring for "likeable" characters in fiction. I don't necessarily root for Undine, but neither do I want to look away. Of all of Wharton's female characters, she's the only one who isn't forced to die or live alone in misery as punishment for going after what she wants. And in her I see something of all of us academic-wannabees: we learn to speak the language, we pretend to understand Foucault, to have strong opinions about obscure

German philosophy, to have read (and adored!) *Ulysses*. But catch me at home on my couch, and you're more likely to see me poring over a weekly celebrity gossip magazine than the latest issue of *The Journal of Literary Criticism*.

Solomon, Isaac. *Get a Life, Get a Job, Get a Better Boyfriend: Implied Words of Wisdom from a Well-Meaning Father.*

When my dad called this weekend, I lied and said we were trying to work things out. Sometimes it's easier to invent stories than to actually look at things for real, especially when I'm talking to a man who is always detecting signs that I'm unhappy: "Is graduate school worth it?" he'll say. "Are you getting enough sleep?" Or: "I hope they're teaching you something interesting because they sure aren't preparing you for the real world."

He sends his regards, by the way. The funny thing is, even though he doesn't say it, I know he finds you unworthy. It's his tone of voice, a kind of icy distance he also adopts when he talks about Mom. For example, he'll tell me how he ran into her and Frank at the grocery store, how she seemed good and looked good and was buying a lot of ribs for a dinner party, but what he'll want to say is how hurtful it is to keep running into the love of his life—the woman who left him the second a more business savvy option came along—at the supermarket. I used to appreciate my father's diplomacy, the fact that he has never derided my mother or chided me for my poor choices in men. He should, though. His quiet acceptance of people's romantic failings is considerate, but it never got him anywhere in his own relationships.

Tilman, Helen. *A Few Things Are Illuminated.*

My mother has a PhD in marine biology, but she runs a daycare center. In her third year in graduate school, she fell in love with her advisor and moved with him for a summer to Mosquito Bay to research phosphorescent plankton. I find this period of her life entirely fascinating and romantic, but she claims she hates talking about it. "I was a cliché," she'll say after enough dry martinis. "Sleeping with my old and married professor. Skinny-dipping at night in the glow-in-the dark Caribbean. Kayaking through luminescent lagoons."

As it turns out, the dude was using her research and not giving her credit. She discovered something about the reproductive processes of dinoflagellates that he passed off as his own find. But she won't talk in detail about what she discovered, because to describe it, she says, would remind her all over again of that sequence of powerful sensations—the wonder of discovery followed by the wound of betrayal.

Roberts, Ralph. *Hard to Get: An Undergraduate Romance.*

Years before you, there was Ralph, the long-distance runner. He wasn't even my type—he was pre-law, wirey, clinical, and distant. We had some good banter going on initially, but our love life was lousy. He refused to kiss me during sex. In that way, he reminded me of a prostitute.

And yet I sat up at night wondering why he hadn't dropped by that day, I called him constantly, I obsessed over whether he thought I was as beautiful as the thin girls on the cross-country team. He never said anything, but I knew he compared. Years later, he married one of them, and I even attended their very lovely and meaningful wedding, but as they danced their first dance I still thought, *Well, fuck you, Ralph. Fuck you.*

Oral Defense

I've been planning what I'll say the next time I see you. I would like it to be something remarkable, something that will make you stagger backwards and put your hand over your eyes because it's just too much to bear.

But instead of eloquent declarations, I'm stuck on this utterly prosaic realization: after you know so much about a person, it's impossible to stop knowing it, no matter how much you wish you could.

Some of our friends have taken up smoking while they write their final chapters. I'm thinking of trying it out—break one horrendous habit with another. Also, I know that if I do start up, you will not try to kiss me again, because even though you like a good Cuban cigar now and then, you hate the taste of tobacco on other people.

By the time I'm on my pack-a-day routine, maybe you'll come over for a beer and we'll joke easily about old times and how I never actually thought you and I were meant to be together. While I dream of a childless lakeside cottage in Slovenia, you secretly want a large and chaotic family that raises chickens and subsists off its own sustainable vegetable garden. You want to be adored by dozens of beautiful and well-read women who love you equally for your tight abs, your puns, and your scholarly articles. You still have a soft spot for the Grateful Dead and yet you look terrible in tie-dye, and when you smoke pot you can't relax; you get tense and start worrying whether you should have gotten your MBA at Harvard like your father thought you would.

Maybe by the next time I see you I'll have decided to move to Italy to study the cooking traditions of a small northern village that has, so far, kept the foreign snoops out. And I'll write a book about my time there, how I really screw up the first batches of polenta, but that by the end of the first year people can't tell which dishes were made by my mentor and lover, and which were made by me. I'll write about winning over the people, about all the offers of marriage I receive, which I turn down of course, because by then I'll have seen how these guys are with their mothers. When the book is made into a blockbuster movie starring Sandra Bullock as me, you'll wish you weren't stuck teaching four sections of freshman composition and one section of introductory French in Grand Forks, North Dakota.

Maybe after I tell you my Italian plans, you'll bring up the Brandy Wine tomatoes you found on your porch swing months earlier. You'll even thank me for them—their fresh flavor will have helped you through a lonely evening. I'll pretend I don't know what you're referring to and suggest that—maybe—you should stop stopping by.

You'll advocate for a continued close friendship, by which you'll mean, let's spend the rest of the day in bed. After all my efforts, you'll overlook the cigarette in my hand because you know it's only a silly prop. And maybe I'll say no. No, we cannot be friends.

But probably I'll just let you lead me upstairs. You'll tug at my sleeve and tell me a joke. I'll be thinking murderous thoughts, but I'll start unbuttoning my blouse as I soften my voice and ask, "So, tell me, where have you been?"

THE CONDOMINIUM

Dave and Emma were supposed to have the beach condo to themselves for a week, but Dave's grandfather showed up on Monday, and it was clear he planned to stay. He owned the place, so Dave and Emma couldn't exactly ask him to scram, but he'd told everyone he would be at his home in Connecticut that entire month, carefully packing up his late wife's belongings and golfing with a senator he planned to support in the next election. Then Dave's uncle Troy arrived two days later, after his wife kicked him out of their house in Coral Gables. Now Dave and Emma had to share the guest bathroom with Troy, who took at least three long showers a day. But the worst thing was how he came into their room at night, after they were in bed.

On Wednesday night, Dave was tugging at Emma's underwear when the guest shower stopped and the bathroom door opened onto their room. The light was off, but the fan still whirred, and the moistness of steam mingled with the crisp, conditioned air. After a pause during which Emma lay rigid under Dave's motionless hand, footsteps came deeper into their room—the nicer guest room that Dave's grandmother had painted seafoam green before she died. For a minute, Dave and Emma closed their eyes and pretended to sleep. Eventually, Troy turned and left, his bare feet making little sound on the carpet.

He came in the next night, too, creeping close enough to touch the bed. In the dull glow of the security lights outside their third-story window, they could make out Troy's arms up in the air, red-handed.

"Hey!" Emma sat up this time and pulled the sheets around her naked torso. "What the hell is your *problem?*"

"Sorry! Sorry!" Troy walked backward, toward the door. "I got confused."

When they heard Troy's own door shut, Emma said, "Do something."

"He's going through a difficult time," Dave whispered.

"So he gets to spy on us every night?"

Dave loved his uncle; he didn't want to make things harder for him. "I'll talk to him. I promise."

It was Thursday night. Emma and Dave would be driving back to Providence on Sunday. In seven days, Emma would move out of their apartment and climb on a plane to San Francisco. Soon after, he would start an internship at his cousin's New York film studio. He felt badly about how the trip was going; he thought he'd planned such a romantic end to their relationship.

He tugged the sheet loose from Emma's body, but she wrapped it more tightly around herself. "I've kind of lost the mood, you know?"

Oh, he knew. Those dark and serious eyes, the way the muscles tensed in her long neck, even though she was smiling at him again. Emma could never hide how she felt, and he loved that about her. Everyone assumed that he was always happy, even when he wasn't.

Except for the little glitch in their condo plans, though,

Dave *was* pretty happy here on the beach with his family. Troy was a problem, but he wasn't *the* problem. Emma had been in a bad mood since they'd decided to pursue their goals on separate coasts. Dave figured that she was waiting for him to suggest they try the long distance thing, but every long distance relationship he knew ended when one person cheated on the other, and he didn't want to wait around for that to happen. Probably what Emma hated most about breaking up was the idea of Dave with someone else. He didn't much like to think of her fucking some California hippy, so he didn't. But Emma turned things over in her mind obsessively. That was why he hadn't told her he planned to stay at Laurel's until he found his own place in Brooklyn. Laurel was so upbeat that it made her seem naïve, even stupid. But of all his friends in New York, she had the biggest apartment.

Emma leaned into him, and he put his arm around her and turned on the television. They didn't own a TV in their place in Providence because Emma had wanted it that way—quieter, less cluttered. He flipped through the channels, then settled on reruns of *The X-Files*, which he and Emma used to watch in his dorm room when she was still dating his buddy Mike, who was studying abroad that semester.

In the morning they woke early. They had no choice: Dave's grandfather was belting out "I Just Called to Say I Love You" in the kitchen while making breakfast. Sizzling bacon had never sounded so loud.

"The lovebirds!" Frank cried, when Emma and Dave emerged in their pajamas.

Emma wore one of Dave's threadbare shirts without a bra, and she had just realized that her shorts gave her a wedgie, but thankfully, Frank did not stare. From what she had observed down here in Miami, he was kind of a dirty old man. Just nine months after his wife's death, the large condo was filled with photos of him and his bikini-clad young girlfriend at resorts in Mexico and Hawaii. Yesterday he'd seemed especially interested in lingering in his parked SUV to watch a clothing-optional photo shoot at Glitter Beach. At least he tried to enjoy his old age, she reasoned, and his wealth.

If her family had that kind of money, maybe she'd be as relaxed as Dave. Who knows, maybe she'd be into golf. Maybe she'd be moving to New York to rent a painting studio instead of to California to work at the advertising agency she'd interned for last summer. She had not loved the work, but it was the only place that gave her a job after graduation. Dave had offered to help with her college loans, but she didn't want to be remembered as the girlfriend he saved from financial ruin.

"Sit! Eat!" Frank gestured to the outdoor patio. His skin was leathery and white chest hairs poked through his guayabera—the only type of shirt he wore down here, procured from a favorite tailor in Cancún. Troy was already outside at the glass-topped table, his back to them.

"Everything smells wonderful." Emma grinned, trying hard to mask her discomfort in the company of these men. She shivered and rubbed her arms. The condo's excessive air conditioning only emphasized for her a sense of forced preservation, the prolonging of a relationship that probably should have ended a long time ago.

Outside, Troy cupped his tanned hand around a mug that read, "Best Grandfather in the World," and did not look up from his paper as they joined him. He wore a button-down shirt unbuttoned over surf shorts.

"Hope you two slept as well as I did," he said.

Emma frowned. "Actually, we were wondering, Troy—"

"Yeah, Troy, we were—" Here, Dave paused, and Emma gave him an encouraging look.

In the pause, Troy had enough time to grab a croissant. With his mouth still full, he said, "I know you guys don't have a lot of time left here. Please say you'll let me take you to the boardwalk. We'll rent rollerblades. I'll buy you lunch."

And then Frank was outside with the bacon. "You can have them for the afternoon, as long as you bring them back before six.

I've made reservations at Donavan's."

"Nana's favorite restaurant," Dave explained. "It's in a classy hotel. Old-timey."

"I beg your pardon," Frank said. "You should see the crowd I run with now."

Dave laughed. He had a lot of heroes, most of them deeply flawed. "There's always some Liberace type playing the Lucite piano. People dancing the foxtrot. Everyone gets very dressed up."

Emma flushed. "I'm not sure I have anything to wear."

Frank sized her up from behind his bifocals. "I'll have Krysta bring something. You're about her size."

Troy frowned. "She's coming?"

"Why do you think I delayed my golfing trip?" Frank smiled at Emma. "Troy disapproves of the age difference." He shrugged. "She's here with her daughter, Rumi, very sweet, who's been shooting a commercial out in LA. Auditioning for some TV pilot." He sighed happily. "A continent between us, but somehow it works."

Emma looked away. She'd heard plenty already about Krysta. Dave was wary of her, but not as wary as the rest of the family, who thought she was after Frank's money. And so what, Emma thought, if Frank wanted to spend his money on youth and beauty. It was an old story, and it was better than being old and alone.

Frank was still looking at her. "You're going to like Krysta, I can tell."

"She's very pretty," Emma said, thinking of the photos inside. It seemed like a safe thing to say.

Ultimately, it didn't matter what she thought of Krysta or her daughter with the name of a male Persian poet, or anyone here. It was time to focus on her new life in San Francisco. Though so many had moved west before her, it still felt thrilling, like an unexplored territory. It also felt a little lonely.

It was June, and although Emma disliked the chill of the air conditioning, out here on the balcony it felt too hot and humid.

Dave loved it. Look at him! With his eyes shut, baking in the patch of sun on his side of the table. Kind, loyal, easy to please. Her heart leapt a little when his green eyes opened and smiled at her.

If only they could be alone for a minute!

Crumbs trailed across the white tablecloth. Troy glared down at his newspaper, muttering to himself. Frank chewed loudly, and Emma looked away, embarrassed. No one seemed interested in keeping up a conversation. She took another piece of bacon. At her house, everyone would be talking, reading aloud from the newspaper, planning the next meal. In the noisy silence, she focused on the clatter of forks on porcelain, on the beach sounds below: the crashing waves and giddy children calling to their parents. Since Tuesday, they'd spent afternoons in the back of Frank's Lexus while he gave them a tour of Miami, pointing out the hotspots, stopping only for sightseeing trips to the aquarium or to let them out to try lox y arroz con moros, his favorite Miami specialty. Today she just wanted to lie on the beach with Dave. He tapped her foot under the table.

"Remember that time we went rollerblading on the bike trail?"

"You tripped over some poor toddler on his tricycle."

Dave winked. "Yeah, that kid was such a klutz."

Emma smiled. For a while she had hoped Dave would ask her to move with him to New York. He didn't have to worry, now; she needed a change. She didn't want to depend on Dave or pine away while he made his indie films and flirted with all the eager, hipster-actresses with their dark fingernail polish and ironic way of smoking.

And she definitely didn't want to go rollerblading. Right now, there was nothing she wanted less.

They went, of course. Troy was the youngest of Dave's mother's four brothers, and he had always been the nicest. Which, in Emma's eyes, might not be saying a lot. One had been indicted for insider trading, and another had recently left his third wife for his family's twenty-two-year-old dogwalker. Troy always seemed different.

When Dave was just a kid and Troy was in college, Troy used to take Dave flying in his grandfather's little waterplane, the one he took between Connecticut and the lake house in Maine. He used to let Dave steer sometimes, which was especially exciting because his mother had said not to do it.

"He can date who he wants," Troy said. He skated backwards, slowly, while Dave and Emma adjusted the rollerblades Troy had rented for them at a nearby skate and surf shop. "But this Krysta is a real con artist, if you ask me. I think she uses the kid to make him feel sorry for her."

"Grampa's no fool."

The boardwalk was now filled with big-hatted tourists, joggers, and power-walkers. Dave caught himself staring at three girls rollerblading by in string-bikinis, their backsides glistening with sweat or tanning oil. He looked at Emma, but she hadn't noticed. She'd given up on the roller blades and was just sitting on the bench next to him, eyes downcast or closed, feet in the skates, latches unlatched. She said his family always talked about money, and he felt embarrassed that it was happening again.

"What else could it be?" Troy asked. "You see the pills he takes every morning? Thanks to western medicine, he can still get his dick up."

"You guys go on ahead," Emma said, tonelessly. "I'll catch up."

"Are you sure?" He felt terrible. He was messing everything up, making all the wrong decisions. They should have gone to a B&B on the Cape instead, like they'd talked about. But he'd thought Emma would appreciate staying somewhere for free, and it really was a beautiful condo, especially on that first day when they'd had it to themselves and didn't leave it once; it hadn't felt like prison then. He thought fondly of the sex they'd had that evening on the sofa, the French doors open and the air conditioning off so they could hear the waves. It already seemed so long ago.

He said, "I'll talk to him, I promise."

"Good."

Her hair was starting to curl loose from her ponytail, the

way it always did in high humidity. He forgot and remembered all the time how lovely she was. Just sitting there, practically vibrating with irritation, she still managed to draw him in. Putting his arm around her, he kissed her hard, right in front of Troy.

As they skated away, Dave wondered what they would both be doing a month from now, three months. He thought of the August garbage smell in New York. Once he and Emma had gone there together in summer, and she'd walked around with her nose in a handkerchief for days.

Back in Providence, she'd said it was the best trip they'd ever taken together.

Emma felt relieved to be left alone. She took off her own sickening-pink blades, and barefoot, walked over to the skate shack.

"They don't fit?" the cute attendant asked. His nametag said *Javier.* "You want a smaller size, probably. You have tiny feet."

"I'd rather walk," she told him, accepting her flip flops.

His short hair was neatly combed, and he wore a white oxford shirt tucked into khakis. Everyone else out here was practically naked. Emma laughed, and Javier did, too, misunderstanding.

He looked at his watch. "Break just started. Mind if I come?"

His question caught her off-guard, but she was feeling annoyed at Dave and Troy, and she liked Javier's formal look, so she said yes.

They walked back to the boardwalk and joined the other pedestrians. Javier was a senior at the University of Miami, majoring in Civil Engineering, something that struck Emma as so useful that when he asked what she did, she was embarrassed to tell him.

"While you repair our country's infrastructure, I'll be designing all those stupid online ads you ask your browser to hide."

Javier shrugged. "Everything has its place."

"We're talking about ads for shampoo and deodorant."

"I don't know about you, but I use those every day."

Emma laughed—no one really believed what she was

doing was important, not even her mother (who still found the idea of the starving artist kind of romantic), but when Javier smiled, his teeth were white and slightly crooked, and Emma looked down at her sunburned feet, suddenly sad.

"Hey, don't worry," Javier said, "everything's going to be okay."

He took her hand very lightly in his, and even though she didn't know him, she felt better. It reminded her of holding her sixth grade boyfriend's hand at recess as they walked around the track together. Light, hopeful, not weighed down. It was a beautiful, blue-sky day, as it had been every day so far, but for the first time, she felt like she was really seeing it. For several minutes, they allowed themselves to move with the crowd, fingertips touching. Together, they passed blindingly white apartment buildings and the grassy, aloe-covered dunes. When a jogger came between them, Emma got pushed ahead in a swell of shirtless men, one who carried a retro boombox tuned to a Whitney Houston song. When she looked back, she could see Javier—small in the crowd, handing a woman the hat he'd accidentally knocked off her head. She stopped to wait for him, but several feet away, Dave and Troy were leaning against a railing, arms around each other. Troy's back was heaving, and he seemed to be crying.

Threading in and out of other pedestrians, Troy railed a little more against Krysta, then Aunt Patricia—whom he suspected of being involved with a younger coworker. She hadn't understood that his own flirtation with the VP the previous year had been nothing. *Nothing.* No physical relationship had come of it, aside from a chaste kiss under the mistletoe at a company Christmas party. But months later, Patricia had found the text messages on his phone— why hadn't he erased them?! He was kicking himself for it now. He adored Patricia. Beautiful, buxom Patty. And his girls! He would have committed suicide years ago if they hadn't come into his life.

Out of nowhere, then, he brought up Emma. "What's *her* deal?" he demanded.

"Her deal?"

"You know, her agenda? Girl's tense."

Dave chuckled awkwardly. Maybe it was the right time to bring up the room issue. "Well, you know, I wanted to talk to—"

"Help!"

Dave looked behind him: Troy tripping over a crushed soda can, Troy falling onto his bare knees. He cried out in pain, and as Dave helped him up, he started to cry. "How the mighty have fallen," he choked out between sobs. Dave had to steady them both against the railing, which is where Emma found them. For the first time on the trip, she looked relaxed. She didn't ask any questions.

On the drive back to Frank's, no one spoke, and when they arrived, Troy stopped the car and didn't get out. Dave experienced a fearful premonition—an image of Troy driving off to the highway and plowing into oncoming traffic on purpose, but Troy smiled, thanked them both for the outing, and headed back out. He needed time to think, he had an appointment with a lawyer, and there were still some things to organize back at the house.

When they opened the door to the condo, icy, silent air washed over them, and it appeared as if they were alone. Dave perked up.

"You want to test out those Jacuzzi jets?"

Emma seemed to be in an agreeable mood. "Sure," she said, "but first you need to clean your uncle's hair out of the tub." She paused. "What did he say, by the way?"

Dave backed into the bathroom, very slowly. "He feels like a jerk."

Emma felt distracted, thinking about Javier. She'd forgotten how nice the world looked after meeting someone you liked: sharper, cleaner, more welcoming. Smiling to herself, she went to the closet. Who cared if she wore her beach sarong to dinner tonight? But here were two unfamiliar items of clothing: a tan sheath and a satiny halter-dress made from a dramatic turquoise fabric. Both were exactly her size.

Holding one up to her in front of the full-length mirror, she thought she heard something, a giggling down the hall, chords of music. The condo was large enough that it was possible that people were there and she just hadn't heard them.

In the bathroom, Dave was kneeling, pouring bubble bath into the water. He looked so earnest that she felt a little guilty about Javier.

"I think your grandfather and Krysta are here. Fooling around."

Dave turned off the taps and the Jacuzzi jets, and behind the drips from the faucet hitting the foaming water, the voices got louder.

And then clapping and Frank's unmistakable cry of joy, "You are a goddess! A goddess!"

Emma sank down on the floor with Dave. The tiles were wet under her knees. "Oh boy."

Dave squeezed her shoulder. "I'm sorry about this, Em. About everything."

"I know." She tucked her head between his neck and shoulder.

"And look at this princess!" Frank shouted.

A little girl laughed. A woman's voice cried, "Ta da!"

Tentatively, Dave and Emma walked into the living room and found Frank on the couch, an audience of one for two figures twirling in long skirts. He beamed at Dave and Emma when he saw them.

"You're just in time for the fashion show."

Krysta and Rumi turned. The girl couldn't be more than seven. She was exceptionally pretty with dark pigtails trailing down the back of her dress, a gauzy pink frock with old-fashioned creampuff shoulders. She smiled at Emma. "Momma bought me a new dress for doing so well on the audition. They said I looked right for the part."

Krysta curtsied in her snug wrap-dress. "I'm afraid I bought myself a little reward as well." On the floor were pink bags full of tissue paper hiding more garments. In person, she was older than Emma had expected. Her skin was clear and bright but creased around her eyes. Strands of gray streaked her black hair, which was cut into a sleek bob, much shorter than in the pictures around the condo.

Frank was right—Emma liked Krysta immediately. She might have just gone on a shopping spree with Frank's money, but she had a sincere smile. "Thanks for bringing the dresses," Emma said. "They're very nice."

"Oh, good, you found them. And please take them home. They don't fit any more." She patted her right hip. "Frank likes steak dinners too much."

Frank stood and wrapped his arm around Krysta's waist. He winked at Dave. "Isn't she something?"

Dave shook Krysta's hand with unusual reticence. The way Frank was twinkling right now, Emma wondered if he was intending to propose to her tonight, in front of all of them.

Rumi spun around again. "It's a very special day," she said. "I can tell we're all going to get along swimmingly." She plugged her nose, waved her free hand, and wiggled her hips, doing the swim and cracking herself up.

Frank patted her head appreciatively. "Drink orders?" he said. "I'll bring them to you on the balcony, and we'll leave for Donovan's when Troy returns from wherever it is he's gone. Hopefully he's keeping himself out of trouble."

At 5:15, Troy still hadn't returned, and they all sat on the balcony, waiting in their pretty frocks and handsome suits. Emma didn't remember Dave packing his navy trousers or the silvery tie she gave him last Christmas, when her cheap but creative gift ideas had run out. Across the rim of his martini glass, he winked at her, and she flushed, smoothing the turquoise skirt of her dress. Rumi giggled at something her mother said to her, then reached out and held Emma's hand. A little breeze came in off the ocean. The trip was turning out to be a good one, after all.

Frank was already a little tipsy, and when he stood, he wobbled. "I'll get refills," he said. "Krysta, did you know Emma was moving to California? Emma, did you know Krysta met her ex-husband on a Buddhist compound near Berkeley? We're not allowed to use the word 'cult.'"

"I'll help you," Dave said, following his grandfather inside.

He shut the French doors behind him and grabbed the tray of empty glasses. His grandfather had always loved his afternoon cocktails, but suddenly his face looked pale, almost dusty.

"Maybe we should wait till we get to Donovan's," Dave suggested. "Before we have any more?" They stood at the liquor cabinet, surveying the options.

"Do you think she's flighty?" Frank said. He made an uncharacteristically helpless gesture with his hands. "Your grandmother was never an impulse shopper." He turned and looked at Dave. Perspiration dotted his brow.

Dave shook his head, confused but relieved to hear his grandmother had not been forgotten. "You're asking what I think of Krysta?"

Frank nodded. "I want to ask her to move here."

At that moment, two things happened at once. The front door burst open, with Troy standing at the entrance shouting, "They're in fucking Paris! With her fucking boyfriend, that little shit!" And Frank crumpled onto the ground.

"My knees gave out," he said. "For God's sake, help me up."

Troy dropped his heavy bags, ran down the hall, and uncle and nephew tried pulling Frank to a standing position but settled on a seated posture when he wouldn't budge. "Keep your head between your knees," Dave insisted.

Troy handed him an ice pack from the freezer to put on his forehead. Frank brushed it aside.

The balcony door opened. "What happened?" Krysta said, rushing over. "Call an ambulance," she told Dave calmly. "Get me some aspirin," she said to Troy. She put her hands—surprisingly thick and stubby, Dave thought—on his grandfather's back, and rubbed, very gently. "He might be having a heart attack."

As Dave dialed 911 on the condo's phone, he watched Emma and Rumi come in from the balcony. Troy passed Krysta two aspirin and a glass of water, which she held up to Frank's lips. The whole, silent process felt oddly ritualistic to Dave. But even in the calm that Krysta imposed on the situation, Rumi started to cry. It was a bold and throaty sob that struck him as practiced, in spite of the suddenness of everything. A show business kid.

Dave spoke to the operator. He told them where to come. Krysta and Troy were lowering his grandfather down to the ground, keeping his airways open. At the edge of the room, Emma had gathered the little girl into her arms. "It's okay," she said into Rumi's hair. "Everything's going to be okay." She wasn't looking at Dave or anyone else as she said it, but he felt good for a second, as if she were talking to him.

In what seemed to be the middle of the night, Emma jolted awake from a dream in which Troy stumbled once again into their room and stood at the foot of their bed—except this time it was her and Javier in it, and Troy looked down at them and said, "Get out."

Eyes still half-closed, she felt certain Troy had been in the room again. The light was on in the bathroom, and she heard the buzzing of an electric razor.

Emma went to nudge Dave, but he wasn't there. She got up, knocked on the bathroom door. No answer. She threw on a shirt and a pair of Dave's boxers, and went to look for him.

What a strange and awful night. Frank's arteries were blocked. He would be in the hospital a few more days, and Krysta was staying with him tonight. Poor, dear Dave. He had cried on the drive home, his head in her lap.

Tiptoeing over the carpet and then the cool slate tiles in the dining area, she made her way to the doorway of Frank's bedroom. Rumi was curled into the corner of Frank's bed, plush comforter tucked beneath her chin, and Dave sat next to her, one hand on the girl's small shoulder as he read from a picture book. He spoke very quietly, but Emma could tell he was doing all the voices: his pitch rose and fell, and his brow furrowed and smoothed as the story progressed.

She went out to the balcony to wait for him and leaned over the railing. The tide was going out, and a couple strolled in a trail of moonlight on the sand below. They were dark silhouettes, holding hands.

The sliding door opened.

When Troy said, "Nice night," she jumped.

His head and face were newly shaven—his scalp was pink and shiny and raw—and it gave him a bitter, menacing look. He leaned over the railing, too, and out of the corner of her eye, it appeared as though he was ducking his head to kiss her.

She backed away, mortified, but he just handed her a drink. "Bourbon," he said, "on the rocks."

She felt like she hated him. She took a sip anyway, and the burn felt good and buttery. "Nice night," she repeated. "Are you kidding?"

He clinked his glass against hers. "We're all alive, aren't we?"

She didn't answer. Below them, the couple was running into the water with their clothes on.

"Crazy kids," Troy said, chuckling. "You gonna say yes?"

Wow, she was tired. Nothing made sense. "Yes to what."

Troy brought his face closer to hers, and she could see the thready, red veins in his cheeks. "Like you don't know." He pressed his finger against her fleshy upper arm, and he left it there for a beat. "My nephew wants to pop the question."

Emma laughed haltingly, but Troy looked serious, and she felt her stomach turn. Had Dave and Troy talked about this while she was asleep? "That's news—" she stopped. Though she was bewildered, she didn't owe this man an answer, so she finished off her drink and turned to go in.

Troy said, "Things like what happened today kind of put things in perspective, know what I mean?"

Emma stopped, her sweaty fingertips leaving little smudges on the glass door. He could be talking about anything—Frank, his own wife and her boyfriend in Paris. Javier, maybe. She tugged open the door, and the cold air slipped out.

Dave was leaving Frank's room, walking toward her. She smiled at him through the glass, and the way he looked—grateful, relieved—she thought maybe Troy was right, though it still didn't make any sense.

Troy was at her back now, his hand on her shoulder, whispering in her ear: "What do you want, Emma?"

She didn't know. Not this. And then Dave was out there with her. With them. He wrapped his arms around her waist. Troy shook the ice in his glass.

"Don't go," Dave said into her hair, into her neck, and still Troy wouldn't leave.

BETTER THAN FINE

Tuesday grew up waiting to change her name, and a month after her eighteenth birthday, she finally got around to it. She pushed the forms and her 285 bucks across the County Clerk's desk. She'd been saving for the past six months, cleaning houses.

The clerk was a thin woman, with light eyebrows penciled in. "You sure, honey? I mean, the name your parents gave you—no offense—kind of leaves more of an impression."

"Just tell me," Tuesday said, "if I filled it all in right."

Leaving the poorly-heated building, she did wonder how she would tell her parents, who she hadn't spoken with since moving in with Luke that spring. They hadn't even met Luke—her father said he wanted to kill him because of the age difference—but eventually they would have to see the person she had become: Ann, a girl who could manage, manage better than them. A girl who lived every day with pretty, well-made things.

Though the name wouldn't be legal and final for another

few weeks, Luke had been calling her Ann in private since two weeks after Marti had introduced them, the first time she'd told anyone what she wanted to be named. The sound of that clean, simple syllable clung even more tightly to her now that she'd paid to file the paperwork. She thought fleetingly of the original Ann, a poised and pretty girl she'd liked in middle school. Her parents once took Tuesday to their glassy house up north, on Lake Ontario. For five blissful days, Tuesday had eaten sandwiches stuffed with roast beef and cheese and stayed up late playing card games on a screened-in porch that overlooked the water, as vast and promising as an ocean. When Ann's family moved to Texas later that summer, Tuesday had cried for days in the room she shared with her two baby brothers.

There was no time to dwell on her now, or to even revel in being Ann officially. There were the groceries to buy for dinner, and a job to get to—cleaning Marti's house, which for several months last fall and winter had functioned as her own. So she darted through the pedestrianized shopping area toward her parked car, the rusted Dodge that Marti had given Tuesday to help her get around better. She never came downtown as a kid, and she walked quickly, warily, even though she and Luke wandered here often. Today the sky hung gray and low, and a bitter wind nipped through the thin fabric of her sweatshirt, but she'd grown accustomed to winters without jackets. She just pulled up her hood and hunched her shoulders.

Luke laughed when she called downtown the city. He called it a shabby college town. He'd lived in Seattle with his ex-wife, and for a little while in London, with an attractive musician whose publicity photos Tuesday once saw on top of Luke's desk when she was still just his house cleaner.

She made her way past cafes and head shops and storefronts that had remained vacant for months. Although many of the stores already had Christmas decorations in the windows, there were few people out shopping on a work day. Those she saw smiled openly at her, but she still kept her hands in her sweatshirt pockets, one fist clasped around her wallet.

Tuesday hated cleaning Marti's house. It was big, old, and filled
with cat hair. Every surface was covered with dusty family photos
and the ceramic bowls and vases that Marti made in her garage. The
place took hours to vacuum and scrub, and Marti did not pay as
well as she should.

But she had been kind to Tuesday in other, essential ways.
Marti's daughter, the youngest of four kids, had been two years
ahead of Tuesday in school and a fellow member of the track and
field team. The two had not been friends, but Marti had watched
Tuesday at track meets and worried about her from afar. As a child,
Tuesday had become accustomed to sideways glances from adults;
she had a reputation as a quiet but persistent bully. (*Impenetrable*
one teacher called her, and Tuesday had liked the sound of that.)
She was not used to *worrying* anyone, so Marti's attentiveness—
snacks after every meet, then dinner invitations and rides to movies,
then little jobs around the house—had come as a surprise.

Marti was supposed to be away today, but her station
wagon idled in the driveway, the engine on, the back of it piled with
boxes of her pottery to take to the downtown store where she sold
her work and Luke sold his intricate stained glass windows, the
kind Tuesday had only imagined before in churches.

Tuesday pushed open the side door, which was always
unlocked. Inside, the radio played tinkling classical music. When
Marti didn't answer her call, Tuesday chose a Top 40 station and
began scrubbing the downstairs bathroom, her least favorite room
because of the kitty litter—the sharp ammonia smell, the way it
caught under her feet. *Her feet*: she'd forgotten again to remove her
shoes at the entrance, and she returned to the door now to trade
her heavy boots for the plastic slippers that Marti kept for her on a
metal shoe rack.

"Here she is," came a muffled voice, "the beautiful Lady
Ann Russell."

Tuesday wobbled as she looked up from her slippered foot:

Marti in the doorway to the kitchen, a hairpin in her mouth, her broad hands twisting her long, gray hair into a bun. The fat old cat Yeats circled Marti's green tights, leaving wisps of fur. She wore a short skirt today under her drapey, wool sweater. Her good sweater, she called it, which meant it had been expensive.

"Hi," Tuesday said. After everything, after today, it still felt strange saying Marti's name—saying any adult's name, really. She rarely even said *Luke* aloud, though she had it in her head a hundred times a day, like a little prayer: *Luke, Luke, thank God for Luke.*

Marti swept in for a vigorous hug, brushing Tuesday's cheek with her fluttery, peacock-feather earrings. "Congratulations, honey," she said. "We should get you a new coat to celebrate. Keep you warm this winter." She clasped her hands around Tuesday's cold fingers, then touched her cheek. Tuesday tensed but allowed herself to be petted.

"Luke already got me one." A belted, ivory coat that he said made her look like a classic film star. But it drew so much attention to itself that she only wore it in his presence and otherwise kept it in her car.

Seeing Marti's frown, Tuesday realized how she sounded— ungrateful, *inelegant.* She worked up a smile. "But thank you. I appreciate it."

Marti smiled faintly, backing into the kitchen. "Help yourself to the vegan brownies that Josie brought over last night. You remember Josie?"

Another of Marti's projects, a mousy pottery apprentice. Tuesday flashed on a particular way Josie had looked at her and Luke holding hands at Marti's 4th of July party: a little sneer on her chapped lips, a mixture of curiosity and disgust. "Yeah," Tuesday said. "I remember."

Marti waved, then the side door creaked open and clicked shut. The station wagon crunched its way down the long, gravel driveway.

Relieved to be alone, Tuesday got back to work, scouring

the toilet and the consistently moldy shower tiles. Now that she was Ann and no longer living at home, or here, in the overheated guest room filled with hundreds of years of dark antiques, she believed she could begin to be more separate and independent. She had a good-enough list of clients. She didn't need so many things from Marti anymore, and though she was grateful, she no longer wanted to be reminded constantly of the long series of generosities, including money for the abortion she'd had last fall. Including the fact that, even after the abortion, Marti hadn't said anything when Tuesday continued sleeping with that skinny thug, Travis, in the canopy bed that had belonged to Marti's grandmother.

At the bathroom door, the yellow tabbies, Fanny and Alexander, meowed before entering, then rubbed against Tuesday's ankles as she bent over the tub. A bright song she liked came on the radio. "Hey, hey," she sang, "hey, hey, hey, hey." When the cats purred, Tuesday sent a note or two in their direction, but otherwise she ignored them.

By the time Tuesday had finished dusting off the surfaces and neatening the piles in Marti's office, it was getting dark outside. Luke would be home soon, and Tuesday rushed to put away the cleaning supplies in the kitchen closet. Marti had not yet returned.

The supermarket was thick with after-work crowds, and as Tuesday pushed her cart through them, she clutched Luke's list in her hand. She was sure she might forget something important. She shopped for Luke all the time now, but sometimes it still felt like a test and that she would fail it.

Finally, pulling into Luke's driveway—her driveway, she reminded herself—she felt relieved. Luke had moved here to escape all the cities he'd known and built this house on a piece of land from which you couldn't see any of the neighbors. The windows glowed, warm and orange, and framed in them she could see his dusky shape moving about the kitchen. As she walked from the car, she looked up at the stars, the tops of the dark pines. The air smelled of woodsmoke, the icy grass crunched beneath her feet.

Inside the mudroom, she set the grocery bags on the slate tiles Luke had found piled up at the county dump. Everything in this house was like that: discoveries, rescued objects. When she first got the job to clean out here, she'd thought it a strange place, made of many different and competing materials—wood and stone and bright, white walls—with corners and angles that were difficult to get the vacuum into. Now she loved the house for its eccentricities—the triangular window seats, the vaulted ceilings, and the loft above the sunlit living room, just big enough for a yoga mat. She understood now what a work of art was and that it was possible to live a life making things, though she hadn't yet decided what she would make, or even if she wanted to. During the day, Luke designed websites at a small agency in town, and in the evenings and on weekends, he worked in his studio, creating his windows of abstract nature scenes—lush ferns and scarlet poppies, close up and radiant. He was teaching Tuesday how to cut and foil the glass, but she preferred to watch him do it.

"Ann," he said when she came in, "baby." He held out a hand to her. His beautiful hands, she thought: ropey and strong. She loved his narrow shoulders, too, and his bright, gray eyes. Sometimes, though, when she'd been away from him for a while, seeing him again startled her. Only then did she see him as others must—an older, slightly worn man. Older than her parents! But unlike them, he'd always taken care of himself. Even in summer, her father looked unwell, his skin pale and flaking. His teeth were crooked and brown.

As they ate, Luke held her hand on top of the table, and she smiled. "I feel good," she said, "like I've actually accomplished something."

"Look how far you've come!"

"You're always saying that." Usually she believed him. But for the first time, the words annoyed her; they sounded like pity. Still, his smile was bright, drawing her closer. She threaded her fingers through his.

"How's Marti these days?"

"Oh, you know." She shrugged.

Luke raised his eyebrows, took a sip of wine. "She can't help it, baby. She's a worrier."

He'd already finished and was watching her continue with her small, delicious forkfuls, pleased at her appetite. She paused, bunched her linen napkin in one fist. When she'd had her last bite, she moved into his lap and finally unzipped her sweatshirt. "Tell her she doesn't need to worry anymore." She pressed her face into his neck. "I'm better than fine."

The next morning was a Saturday, and as she woke she blearily pushed her hands through the duvet, looking for the warmth of Luke's skin, but he was gone, out in his studio. She had not known a restful sleep until she'd moved in here, and now the thought of her dark and crowded bedroom at home—the way it often smelled of pee when her brothers were still wetting their small cots—made her cringe.

She smelled fried eggs and bacon, which Luke would have made for her. And coffee, which she pretended to be developing a taste for.

She decided to stay in bed. She did it so rarely, and it was one of the great joys in her life, lying alone and naked under the soft, white comforter, staring up and through the skylight. Looking at Luke's stained glass windows gave her a similar feeling. Right now he was working on one just for her: a bright series of lulling, overlapping waves, each wave a slightly different shade of blue.

Vaguely, she registered the phone ringing down in the kitchen.

On the machine, it was Marti's voice. "Tuesday, sweetie, please call when you have a second. Just wanted to talk about—oh, sorry, *Ann*, gosh this is gonna be an adjustment for me." There was a long, breathy pause. "I really hope you'll call. I promise I'm not mad."

Tuesday sat up. Mad? A little, squirmy ball had already started to form in the pit of her stomach, that knot she got when preparing to be wronged. "Shit, Marti," she said to the air. "I'm not calling on my day off."

She flopped back down in bed and tried to revel in the

pillowy mattress and the cloudless sky above, but the spell was already undone. She showered, dressed, and microwaved her cold plate of breakfast. Still feeling tense, she set about her Saturday routine, the chores she had selected for herself so she could continue feeling useful to the running of the house: laundry, dishes, driving into town to get the *Times,* so Luke could later do the crossword puzzle and she could sit on the couch with his arm around her while he did it.

When she returned, Luke was in the kitchen, topping off his coffee. Though he smiled, he seemed to be surveying her as if from very far away.

"Baby, Marti called."

"Yeah, I heard the message."

"No, I mean she called again, I just talked with her."

She began wiping down the kitchen island, where Luke chopped vegetables every night, where he'd first kissed her, leaning her against the wood surface, doing everything she asked.

"Thing is, Ann, Marti had some cash? Sounds like quite a lot of it—over five hundred bucks from that art fair in Syracuse. Sitting on her desk in the office? And now it's gone."

"Why would anyone leave money like that lying around?"

She knew it wasn't the right thing to say as soon as she saw Luke's disappointed face coming toward her. His eyes drooped disapprovingly, the corners of his lips pinched in. His hands were on her shoulders now, pressing down—gently but firmly, gently but firmly.

That little knot of anger was starting to unravel. She brought her hands to her mouth and blew, as if to warm them, when really she was just trying to keep herself from yelling. Marti's fucking office! The stacks of bills, of loose sketches, of last year's Christmas cards, and bags of chocolate candies Tuesday had to dust around.

"Why would I take Marti's money?" She spaced the words out, hating Luke's coffee breaths on her face. And even then, she wanted to kiss him, wanted him to clasp his hands—with those invisible shards of glass embedded in the pads of his fingers—

around the small of her back, under her shirt.

"You forked over a lot of your hard-earned money yesterday. That must have been hard."

"You don't wait your whole life to do something, just to find out it's easy."

"Baby, honey, we understand. We're not mad. We know what you've been through."

We. And just like that, she was on the outside again. He might as well have handed her a check for all her very hard work.

She had sometimes taunted classmates on the playground or left cruel notes in the lockers of girls she did not like. Every day, she had pretended not to know her own mother, who worked in the high school cafeteria and served Tuesday her reduced-price meals. But she had never taken what didn't belong to her.

"It was Josie." Her voice was calm with certainty. Picturing the girl's calculating sneer, Tuesday felt beyond reproach.

But something shifted and settled in Luke's expression. "Oh, honey," he said.

"You don't believe me."

"I just think—" He stopped. "Josie has her own problems."

"Obviously!"

When she tried moving, he tightened his grip on her. "Don't go, Ann. Don't run away."

Now that's all she wanted to do! She pushed hard on his chest, and he stumbled backwards, gazing at her with surprise.

At the door, she turned. Luke was a tall man, but he looked small and winded.

Outside, she managed to get her icy hands on the wheel and turn the car around, her heart thumping. Underneath her anxiety, she felt something new—a sense of release suspended just below the surface. For hours, she drove on back roads until the moon cast a bluish tint to all the little hills and houses. She felt like she was being forced to make a big decision about the direction of her life, because how could she go back to Luke if this is how he saw her—a troubled little thief?

Just think how far you've come! Tuesday laughed. At least her parents had left her alone.

Turning onto her old road, she passed the gravel pit and that big old house she'd loved as a kid but which looked out of place now that it had been painted a lurid shade of lavender, as if it were on a tropical island or among those gingerbread houses she'd seen photographs of in San Francisco, where Luke had also lived, in his twenties. And then came the individual mobile homes on big parcels of land—first Dawn and Robbie's with that ugly little gazebo still falling down in the front yard, then Patrick's tidy double-wide with its above ground pool she and her friends had snuck into as kids. And then her trailer park. Here was Jackie bending with a plastic sack of groceries, the interior light of her two-door sedan still on. Tuesday waved and Jackie waved back, then ducked quickly inside, probably to call someone, probably Tuesday's mother. And here was Angela's old trailer, dark and empty-looking and rusted, cinder blocks and two old bikes piled on a blue tarp in the front yard. Last Tuesday knew, Angela had followed a guy to South Carolina, and her mother and youngest brother went soon after.

When she got to her house, she had to sit in the car for a minute before turning off the engine. There was a small porch now, strung with blue and red Christmas lights. Her father or JC must have put up the porch over the summer, because before there had been nothing, just the door, and then a drop.

Luke's coat, the coat he'd bought her, lay across the passenger seat, and she put it on before she went in. She didn't have to knock, her mother was already at the door, eyeglasses nesting in the white-blonde poof of her hair. Tuesday just stood on the tiny porch for a second with the cold air billowing around her, aware suddenly of all her limbs and the heavy feel of the wool on her wrists. And then her mother smiled, looking Tuesday up and down.

"Tu-tu," she said, opening her arms. She wore her familiar black sweatpants and a pink T-shirt, stretched tight across her large chest. It was sheer enough that Tuesday could see the soft rolls of flesh above the elastic of the waistband. When they hugged, Tuesday went slack, feeling a mixture of relief and revulsion. And humiliation—she'd left home pregnant, angry, and unemployed, and look at her now! What did she have to brag about, except that she had a different name, and this fancy coat she never really wore?

Inside, she kept the coat on and didn't sit down. There was the smell of pizza, and under that, the faint odor of burning plastic. She might as well have left here only days before. No one got up to make a fuss. The television was on, and the lights were dim, the way Tuesday's father liked it.

He sat in his recliner, drinking an orange soda, his bad leg a bony stick emerging from the ends of his pajama pants. JC and Bobby were on the brown couch, the only other piece of furniture in the room, aside from a tinny space heater, clicking away near her father's feet.

"Huh," her father said, "look who's home for the holidays." He raised the can. "Left that old fucking hippy?"

She smiled nervously. "Just stopping by, Daddy."

A small Christmas tree blinked in the corner, and atop it teetered the clothespin angel she'd made in kindergarten, its long, yellow-yarn hair still pristine and straight.

"Cut that down along the old railroad tracks," JC said, nodding at the tree. "You know, how we used to do?"

"You guys complained about that fake tree," her mother said, "but I liked how it didn't drop any needles." She pointed underneath the tree. "What a mess!"

She went to the microwave and returned with a bowl of soup. "Here, sit!" Placing the minestrone in Tuesday's hands, a little of it sloshed over the side and onto her coat. Served her right, she thought, for never wearing it.

She sat next to JC and spooned canned minestrone into her mouth, feeling starved. This was the kind of food Luke teased her for still liking, when he said he'd cook her anything she wanted and she still asked for Chef Boyardee. Her mother perched on the arm of the couch, one hand resting lightly on the top of Tuesday's head.

For a little while, they all just sat around like that, watching a rerun of *Quantum Leap*. Instead of really watching it, she kept rubbing at the new stain on her coat, wondering what Luke was doing. Worrying, probably. Talking to Marti on the phone or shopping for glass online. She thought of calling to reassure him, but she didn't want everyone listening to their conversation.

At some point, she must have fallen asleep. The television was still on with the volume muted, and she lay alone on the couch, a thin blanket tucked under her chin. Her cheeks felt cold, but she still had her coat on, and all her limbs were warm enough. Her mother came out from the bathroom, her bathrobe loosely tied. She'd always had trouble sleeping through the night.

"It's snowing," she said. She knelt on the ground next to Tuesday. "You need to be careful on the road in the morning."

Tuesday nodded. Hot tears sprung into her eyes.

"Where you going, baby? You can tell me."

How quickly her future was unfolding! She saw it clearly, all at once: painting the rooms of her rented cottage near the water, cleaning houses in the summer for vacationers, and pouring coffee for the locals in the little diner where she had eaten pancakes with Ann's family. "The lake, Momma."

It sounded crazy—driving north in this weather?

But her mother just said, "You need some money?" She fished into the pocket of her robe and handed Tuesday a neat pile of cash.

Tuesday didn't know if her father was working. Even when he was, there had never been any extra money at the end of the month. When Tuesday had come to them, pregnant and afraid, her father had said, "We figured it out, so I guess you'll have to."

Without counting the bills, Tuesday wrapped her fist around them and closed her eyes.

For a long time, her mother just stayed on the ground, her back against the sofa, and she fell asleep sitting up. Tuesday couldn't sleep and didn't want to, now that she had a plan.

Except for her mother's rabbity snores, everything was quiet: a wintery silence that made a person think better, that felt like an opening. It was still dark when Ann crept out the door.

SOME OF US CAN LEAVE

People say your life flashes before your eyes right before you
die, but it also happens when you find out you're pregnant. And
unemployed. First, Bethany fired me between Mrs. Temple's
mani-pedi and lip wax. Five minutes later I was in the Nifty Nails
bathroom, staring at a little plus sign and feeling sick about my life.

Even though I did the prettiest acrylic nails of all the girls,
I still made clients nervous. Bethany said, "Instead of just scrubbing
their bunions, you make them feel ashamed." It's true I sometimes
point out when a woman has let her feet go, but I explained it's
for the women's own benefit. Bethany looked at me sternly. "Mrs.
Temple's seventy-seven. She doesn't need to hear that she can't pull
off a pair of strappy sandals."

With all the aromatherapy candles and soft lighting, the
bathroom at Nifty Nails is designed to make bad things look better.
Well, I sat on the heated toilet-seat, wondering how to tell Bill the
day's news, and it turns out the future doesn't look any better with

mood lighting.

Someone rapped on the door. "Liz, honey?" It was Bethany. "Can you come out here and do Mrs. Temple's wax?"

"I thought I was fired?"

"After the lip wax."

I tried to think of a snappy response, but nothing came.

For the last time, I flushed that spotless toilet. Then I removed Mrs. Temple's unwanted mustache without looking her in the eye. Leaving Nifty Nails with my nail kit under my arm, I walked quickly, as if I had somewhere better to go.

Bill's reaction this morning surprised me. "Let's go on a picnic."

"You're happy?" I asked.

"Why, aren't you?" He started dancing me around the kitchen. "Now you can stay at home and get in Mommy mode."

I'm not sure that's something to celebrate. But here we are at the park where we had our first date. We were sixteen then. A wave of nausea hits me as we head toward the lake. I'm carrying the plastic lawn chairs while he drags the cooler in the Red Flyer wagon and yammers. He's already decided on a name, a face, and a responsibility on future family picnics: Mark Joseph after Bill's father. Freckles and green eyes like me. Sandwich-maker and wagon-puller.

My head has grown a layer of mold. The water looks so far away. The beer cans tap against each other and the ice in the cooler, and the wagon wheels rattle along the ground. I rarely notice such unimportant sounds, but now every little thing is magnified. I try focusing on the sounds and not on my discomfort.

Bill stops walking. "You look like a bad hangover, Lizzie."

I stare at his paunch. His beer gut is so rounded and taut that he looks like a woman starting her third trimester.

"Fat around the middle," I sing-song, "is a recipe for heart disease."

"Nice, Lizzie." He strides away, muttering to himself and perhaps to his vision of our future child, unwilling puller of wagons.

We find a shady place under a willow tree. I slump into my lawn chair, hoping I won't puke in front of all the other picnickers. From behind his aviator glasses, Bill watches the lake. "You know," he says, "I'm starting that protein diet tomorrow."

"Go for it," I say. "Live a little."

"Bud and Lorna like it."

"Ah, Pudge and Lovehandles." I know I'm being mean.

I nibble on a corn chip and swallow a mouthful of cola. I can't get comfortable; the plastic mesh of the chair pinches my butt. As a Nail Specialist, I had a steady hand, but now my fingers tremble as they massage my belly. Losing my job was probably for the best; I'm sure those fumes are terrible for a fetus. But how is staying home gonna help with the car payments? Bill works under the table for this asshole who doesn't invest in any safety gear—no hard hats or secure scaffolding and definitely not health insurance for his employees.

From the corner of my eye, I watch Bill breathe unevenly, drinking from the can. He's already an insomniac, and the early mornings shingling the Harringtons' roof have him running on even less sleep. So it was nice to see him perk up when I told him. I actually felt a little excited, too. But then his enthusiasm only reminded me that this was the rest of my life: nothing more than this man, our baby, this whole business of getting by in the middle of nowhere.

When my life flashed in the Nifty Nails bathroom, I can't say I saw very much. The last time we were anywhere except this park was Niagara Falls in June, probably where I got pregnant. It was our annual tour on the Maid of the Mist. Bill works with a guy who knows a travel agent who gets us a discount on tickets, so it's become this thing we do that everyone knows about. "You and Bill doing your thing this year?" my mother asks. Bill and I have tried inviting her and my dad, but she says they don't want to impose. The truth is, she's afraid of boats. She grew up around the Finger Lakes, and she never learned how to swim.

On our most recent trip, Bill started talking to the only guy not wearing one of the blue ponchos the tour center passed out as we boarded. "You are going to get fucking soaked, my friend," Bill said, pointing at the nicely dressed dude. I elbowed Bill. He knows I hate when he swears in front of strangers. The guy shrugged. "You were fucking right," he said to Bill later, and the two of them just cracked up over the guy's water-logged loafers. His wife, blonde and pretty underneath her poncho, smiled and ran her hand up and down her husband's damp arm. Over drinks at the hotel bar, we learned that they were childless and in love. They'd been all over the world: Asia, Europe, Alaska. They saw museums and plays. Once, my sister and I went to see *The Lion King* in New York, and I was blown away. Blown away, I tell you.

Back in our room that night, I asked Bill, "Why don't we go to China or something?"

He looked at me like I was crazy and held up a finger, the stumpy one he cut off with the band saw in tenth grade—seven years ago now. "We saw an awesome force of nature today, Babe." He raised another finger. "You tell me where we'll find that kind of thing in China." Then he waved his one and a half fingers around in the air in a little finger victory dance.

From my seat in the shade, I spot a young couple on a bench near the water—blonde ponytail and fake tan on her, baseball cap and desperate, horn-dog look on him. The girl's arm is around the guy's waist, and he whispers in her ear and then bites her earlobe, playfully. She starts giggling like the teenager she is. I wish my mother had sat me down when I was young and asked me what I wanted out of life. But I'm not sure anyone asked her either, and she seems happy to go along with what she's been offered: a husband with steady work, three kids who call or visit every weekend, a garden big enough for all her sunflowers. In seventh grade, my art teacher, Miss B, told me I had talent, and I believed for that entire year I might one day become a famous painter. Then Miss B married the biology teacher with terrible breath, moved to New

Mexico, and I never drew another thing. After I graduated from high school, Bill's sister Lorna thought I might like doing nails at Bethany's spa. "Because you're artistic," she said. Lorna even helped me find a cheap nail tech course at the community college. And look how I pay her back—by pissing off old ladies and calling her names behind her back.

Up the shore, a bunch of seagulls chases after bits of food that a barbecuing family tosses. A toddler, off-balance, shrieks and runs away from the flapping wings. Crying, he falls into the grass. Bill stares at the boy, grinning. "Kid's gonna be a ball player." I squint at him. I can't tell if he's talking about the toddler or our unborn child.

Offering me a beer, Bill says, "I like it here."

I scowl and wave away the can.

Bill nods. "Sorry. Got lost in the moment."

I wish I could get lost, too. The weather is fine. This park is perfectly nice. I have nothing against kids. Everyone assumed we would be popping them out right after the wedding, but for three years that didn't happen, and after a while I figured one of us was infertile. Bill's mother cried sometimes, because no one was giving her grandchildren, but I felt relieved. I never went back on the pill.

I listen to car doors shutting, engines starting and driving away from the park. I put the cool beer can against my forehead.

Bill pulls my hand toward him, and our forearms hover over the grass. He's not a bad guy. I'm not always easy to deal with.

I smell charcoal and burning hot dogs. I feel my pulse in my ankles, like a tiny frog jumping under the skin. When I close my eyes, I hear the jangle of a dog's collar as it shakes itself off after a swim. My elbow aches from digging into the plastic armrest, so I focus on the water lapping on the rocks. I focus on the splash of a kayaker's paddles.

Then I focus so hard on the rustling wind in the leaves that I become the wind for a second, if that makes any sense. As I listen to the jabbering seagulls, things get even stranger: One minute I'm sitting beside Bill, the next I'm flying with those birds, looking at the shadows between their feathers. From above myself I can see my ugly expression, a grimace on a sweaty face. I hear Bill planning our family vacations at the amusement park at Darrien Lake. "We'll take the camper!"

Near the high branches, there's a nice breeze off the water. Patches of leaves have turned orange already. My earthly body disappears as I rise into the clouds, thinking I should be cold and scared but feeling only a sense of warm weightlessness. And then I float. No echoes, no voices. Just dark and dark and dark, illuminated by a brilliant sphere that holds both me and Bill and the people grilling their burgers on the shore, as well as all the houses on the lake and all the farms and gorges and nail salons in the county.

The earth is a pearl: radiant, spinning. I think of the billions of people walking on its surface—grandparents, parents, children. Wars and birthday parties happening at once, cars driving over roads once traveled by covered wagons, malls being expanded while people tend their gardens. As I hover, gazillions of bare feet tread on grass at tranquil parks, bazillions of little fists clutch at corners of furniture to steady themselves, and a chorus of voices shout, sing, and whisper their prayers.

Gradually I sense myself retreating further, deeper into space. Assuming I'll see other planets in orbit, I look around me and see nothing, not even my own hands waving in front of my face. Finally, I relax. At some point I imagine I'll return to earth, buy ugly maternity jeans, and see a doctor at the walk-in clinic. But right now, those concerns are small and I am vast. From here I can see myself sometime along in years, passing out of the world with millions of other bodies at the same time. Some of us leaving people behind, some of us just leaving.

SAY SOMETHING NICE ABOUT ME

After six years together, I told Gregory, "If we don't have a kid, I'm leaving." He worried about overpopulating the earth, but I knew he feared being alone more. So we had this ravenous infant, a fitful sleeper. I was sure the marriage wouldn't last anyway.

Naomi was almost ten months old when I invited my college roommate and her fiancé down from Toronto. I was unhappy in Helena but didn't say so. Instead I said I wanted to meet her man before the wedding. I wanted them to see my beautiful girl. My life felt unremarkable in most ways, but having a baby still seemed like an accomplishment worth bragging about.

Kim's silkscreens of densely populated cityscapes were hanging in corporate offices all around North America, but she rarely talked about her own accomplishments. Even so, Gregory had never thought she was as fun or talented as I did. He was not thrilled about the visit, but at least he was willing to watch Naomi crawl through the unkempt grass in the backyard while I put clean sheets on the guestroom bed.

"She's not very coordinated," he said when I came outside. The air was humid, and the tall maples surrounding our house were still. "Grace and Jerry's kid is already walking, and Naomi doesn't even crawl right."

"She's a baby, Greg. She'll figure it out."

Hands on his thin hips, he watched our daughter move unsteadily toward a patch of tangled dandelions, kicking her right leg to the side like an injured flipper, then collapsing under the weight of her chubby arms. For a second, she seemed to disappear, swallowed by the tall grass.

"I hope so," Gregory said. He shook his head, hopeless, as Naomi began to work herself into a cry.

Gregory had a knack for seeing the dark side of things, and he only seemed to get better at it after Naomi was born, once we had something real to worry about. I couldn't remember the last time we'd had guests or lighthearted conversation. The shapely upstate New York landscape had delighted me in college and made me swear I'd never return to the flatlands of the Midwest, but it felt isolating now, free as it was from good public transportation or a truly serviceable airport that might have attracted more far-flung company. Just before Naomi's birth, I'd quit my job as manager at a "jewelry" store downtown. I didn't miss it. I'd never considered crystals or dream catchers to be precious gems, so it was difficult to get enthusiastic about the merchandise. But my old dream of having my own business—a bookstore and coffee bar—seemed far away and impractical now. There was the baby, of course, but also our mortgage and the debt we'd incurred from a flooded basement that spring. We owned just one car, and Gregory needed it to take clients to see the houses that they rarely ended up buying from him.

When the silver BMW pulled into our driveway, I began having second thoughts about the visit. Kim and Freddie, a significantly older otolaryngologist from Arizona, were all over each other the moment they got out of the car.

"My soul mate," is how Kim introduced him.

"*Mon amour,*" Freddie said, making out with her on the splintered porch step that Gregory was supposed to have replaced before our visitors' arrival.

I was a little embarrassed by the display. Jealous, too. And annoyed at myself for feeling unkind. When Kim finally detached from Freddie to hug me, she smelled like tea roses, her old perfume. "I'm so glad you're here," I said, trying hard to mean it.

Kim plucked Naomi from my arms. "The whole drive down," she said, "I couldn't wait to get my hands on her!" Looking Naomi in the face, she laughed. "I knew your mother before she was responsible, kiddo."

Naomi did not appear amused. Pressed to Kim's narrow chest, she kept reaching for me, watery eyes pleading, and I found myself mildly satisfied that, given a choice, she still preferred me.

"Let Auntie Kim hold you," I said benevolently. "She's come all this way."

I couldn't get over how tan they both were, even though they lived in Canada now. Once pale and soft, Kim had become taut-skinned and athletic.

We hadn't seen Kim since the Reagan administration—my least favorite presidency but some of the happiest years of my life. Kim and I were scraping together rent for our small apartment and skipping classes and dreaming of a future rich with friends, travel, and romance. Outwardly, I complained about supply side economics and where the country was headed, but every night when Kim and I got together in the kitchen over homemade pasta, the world still felt full of possibility.

Back then, Kim wore the same long skirt day after day after day; she kept her hair long and wild. She looked harder as a young preppy, less approachable. I wondered what she thought about the differences in me: my hair was going prematurely gray, and I had purple crescents under my eyes, like permanent makeup. Kim winked at Freddie and reached up a hand to fluff her perm. In college, I'd been the vainer one, sleeping in rollers and cold cream.

I grinned hard and tucked a frizzy strand of hair behind an ear. I wanted her to tell me I looked good, even though I didn't. I wanted her to see through my forced cheer, shuttle me into a quiet corner of the house, and tell me what to do with my marriage. She'd always had such a good sense of direction and an instinct for joy. But she was busy examining the untended yard and rotting porch. "It's charming!" she cried, unconvincingly. "A little house on the prairie!"

"*Absolument!*" Freddie pulled Kim to him and reached for Naomi, who went to him without a fuss. She yanked on the turquoise beads around his neck. For several seconds, I was stunned by how natural they looked together. Naomi turned her head once to locate me, then seemed to forget my existence.

Something odd was coming over me—static in my brain, a cool vice gripping my chest. I felt untethered from the moment, watching from above as I slipped inside to spike some lemonade for everyone of drinking age.

Returning to the porch with a silvery tray of clinking glasses, I wanted to blame Gregory: his even complexion had gone mottled, and he had that withdrawn, hunched-shoulder look that meant he was retreating into himself.

It made me want to shake him. Just after we got married, we went camping together in the Adirondacks, and we pitched a tent right on the shore of the lake. It was a hot and sticky day, and Gregory and I had stripped down quickly and flung ourselves into the water with a kind of unabashed pleasure I barely connected to the man in front of me. He hadn't touched me in days. In bed he'd begun wearing pajamas again, as if for protection. If I had put my arm around him then, he would have slunk away from me, claiming it was too hot. So I grabbed Naomi—sticky and in need of a diaper change—because I wanted something to hold on to.

She only had eyes for Freddie now, but I didn't let her go to him, and she started to whimper. She would be wailing any second.

Gregory looked at the suitcases that had been dropped by the stairs. "You guys must be tired after the drive," he said. I could tell he wanted to take a nap. Lately he'd been sleeping more during the day than Naomi. "We can get your bags inside, and then maybe we'll all have a little rest."

He spoke without really looking at anyone—focused instead on the bags, the door, his near and distant future. Anything but any of us.

Gregory was tired, Naomi was tired, I was tired. Kim and Freddie weren't tired. It was only a six-hour drive, and Freddie loved to drive! I thought it would be nice if Kim and I took a quiet walk together and suggested it, but Freddie said he wanted to see the campus.

Kim agreed. "We have such a short time here," she said. "Let's show Freddie where we got schooled."

They changed clothes—a sleeveless, flowered dress for Kim, a new, white polo for Freddie—and Gregory loaded the carseat in the BMW. I got to the silky car and saw myself reflected in the tinted window—my sweet-potato-splattered t-shirt and the hair that aged me—so I ran back to the house and threw on a linen dress and a straw hat that I bought for gardening but that made me feel, on my good days and with the right pair of sunglasses, like a poor man's Grace Kelly.

Naomi cried the entire twenty-minute drive to the scenic expanse of campus, where, as students, we had come to watch the sun set over the lake.

"Make-out central, I bet," Freddie said. "You bring all your boyfriends here, Kimmie?"

"Only the lucky ones," Kim said.

"So consider yourself lucky," Gregory said, sounding mean.

Freddie didn't seem to notice. "Oh, I do! *C'est ça, C'est ça, C'est ça!*"

He grabbed Kim's hand, and together, they ran down the grassy hill.

"What a self-absorbed ass," Gregory said.

"He seems nice." I shaded my eyes so I could better see Freddie and Kim embracing and laughing, falling to the grass and tickling each other.

"What's so nice about him?"

"He loves her."

"He loves fucking a younger woman."

Freddie was walking on his hands now. He looked honestly ridiculous, but I was impressed that a fifty-year-old had that kind of stamina.

"You have to admit that he's spontaneous." I said it sarcastically on purpose, and Gregory chuckled. It was uniting to share disdain for a person, even if I was only pretending to be disdainful.

"He keeps his whites white."

"A passable French accent."

"You get a raisin stuck in your ear, he could get it out, no problem."

"Sinus infection, and he's your man."

"He's rich. He's successful. He drives a nice car with real leather interior." Gregory's voice was still playful, but I heard the sadness creeping in. "He probably carries one of those mobile phones in his glove box."

I squeezed his hand, and he squeezed back.

Hope, affection, good humor—I thought these things mattered to me most. Even though the drive in Freddie's car had been seductively smooth, it wasn't something I longed for. Not really. I had reasonable expectations for comfort: a roof, sturdy walls. In the winter, I didn't mind piling on the sweaters. I might never have my own bookstore, but when Naomi was old enough to go to school, I would head back to work. Eventually, I knew we would be able to afford a car with under 100,000 miles. For the time being, Gregory was still trying to figure out if he was going to be a real estate agent or a social worker. He was leaning toward real estate, which he wasn't very good at, but he volunteered at a suicide prevention hotline one night a week, just to see how it made him feel. He did not say so, but I guessed it was a relief to talk to people who felt sadder than him.

He turned to Naomi, and in his gaze I recognized both his longing to connect with her and his fear of doing so. To reach out, both loving and needy, and then to be rejected—I knew there were few things more terrifying to him.

He patted Naomi's head gingerly, awkwardly, and at his touch, she started to fuss. When he took away his hand, he looked pained.

"I upset her," he said.

"I need to change her diaper. She's probably hungry."

Whatever the moment had been, it was gone. If I left Gregory now, I wondered, where would I go? Gregory stuffed his hands in his pockets.

Kim and Freddie were walking up the hill toward us, their faces flushed and cheerful, and I felt that tightness in my chest again. I tried to concentrate on the way things used to be with Kim, how just seeing her walk in the door to our apartment made me happy. When things weren't working out with a man or a job, she would tell me it was probably for the best and that something better would come along: "Only the best for you, Mir. The best for the best."

We ate at the old vegetarian restaurant on campus, and Kim was delighted that it had retained its former shabbiness, but Gregory remained unimpressed. He'd never been a fan, even in its heyday.

"You're not going to convert carnivores with dusty floors and sticky menus." He sniffed. "Smells like BO in here."

He was right, but I got defensive. "They do amazing things with tofu."

Freddie smiled at Gregory. "I used to hate tofu, too, *mon ami*, until I met Kim." He was rubbing her leg under the table. "She's opened me up to the possibilities of things."

Naomi, meanwhile, was gazing rapturously at Freddie from her high chair. "I think she likes you, Freddie," Kim said.

"Hey little darlin'," he said, addressing Naomi in a baby voice. "Am I your new best friend?"

Gregory and I had agreed not to use the baby voice with

Naomi. But when Gregory talked to her—if he talked to her—
he spoke with a strange blend of caution and condescension, as
if he were having a conversation with one of his hotline clients,
counseling her against swallowing the entire bottle of baby aspirin.

Naomi seemed to like the baby voice; she giggled, and her
pacifier fell out of her mouth.

"She looks like you, Greg," Kim said. "She's a beauty, even
with no hair. I usually don't like bald babies."

"She looks like my mother," Gregory said.

Freddie said, "I think she looks like Miriam."

"She looks like herself," I said, rather stupidly. But I
couldn't help it; it's what was taking shape for me: this future
person distinct from all other people, who one day—very soon,
right this minute—would separate herself from those responsible
for her being in the world.

And then where would I be? Like Gregory, I realized, I did
not want to be alone.

I wanted to tell him: we are both afraid. But Gregory wasn't
looking at me. He was telling the waitress he wanted fresh spring
rolls, and he was apologizing for Naomi, who was shrieking with
glee after having gotten a hold of someone's fork and knife and sent
them clattering to the floor. He was saying to Kim and Freddie, "I'm
sorry. I'm sorry."

"We're fine," Kim said, looking at Freddie.

"They're fine," I said, tensely. "This is just how she eats."

"She's doing very well, I think," Freddie said. He caught my
eye and smiled kindly.

When the food arrived, no one said anything for a while;
we just watched Naomi shoveling fistfuls of peas into her mouth
and throwing them on the floor when she tired of them.

"Everyone loves a baby!" the waitress said, annoyed.

Together, she and I kneeled, plucking peas from the floor.
I wanted to tell her to get a broom, for god's sake. She had long,
fragrant dreadlocks, and a shirt that kept slipping off one shoulder.
I hated white-girl dreadlocks. I felt myself sinking into a dark place.

The whole time, the girl—probably a student at my alma mater—muttered curse words under her breath. In my day, the waitresses here had been high but always polite. She did not even seem to notice that I was on the ground with her, helping, getting my nice dress dusty, or that everyone else was still eating and gazing with interest at her cleavage, which was substantial, and not constrained by a bra.

I hoped to finally get Kim to myself after putting Naomi to bed, but when I came back downstairs, Freddie was pouring bourbon for everyone and setting up a slide projector he'd packed in one of the suitcases.

"Slide show!" Kim said, laughing, already drunk. Her bare feet were on the coffee table, crossed at her bony ankles. "We want to show you guys our house and our camping trip up north. Where Freddie proposed."

Apparently, Freddie was having trouble with the projector. The light wasn't working or something.

"Piece of shit," he said, kicking uselessly at the floor.

"Hon." Kim got up and rubbed his shoulders. Freddie slumped into his chair in a posture of surrender.

"Hey," Gregory said, "don't worry about it." He raised his glass and took a drink, rallying at this sign of Freddie's weakness. "It's been a great night."

Freddie smirked. "Guess you two don't get out much."

Kim said, "Freddie, hush."

"What are you saying?" Gregory's voice tensed. "We don't know how to have a good time?"

Freddie held his hand in front of his body, as if Gregory were trying to touch him. "Hey, you have responsibilities. *Je comprends.*"

"Do you really?" Gregory said. "Understand, I mean."

I'd been sitting down all this time, and I stood now and took Gregory's hand. "It's getting late," I said. "We've had a lot to drink."

In my hand, Gregory's fingers were rigid.

Freddie said, "Oh, I do understand, *mon ami*. We all, how do you say, *let things slide*."

Gregory laughed. "*How do you say?*'" He turned to me, his eyes watering. "You hear that, Mir? Like English is his second language."

I was trying not to laugh myself, but I didn't want a fight. "Why don't we try the slide show again in the morning?"

I turned to go then, but Freddie reached for my hand and kissed it. I pulled back, surprised. "I only say all this," Freddie said, "because you deserve the best, Miriam. The life of a queen."

My face flushed. It was the kind of declaration I'd wanted to hear, but coming from Freddie, it sounded ridiculous.

Kim whispered something in Freddie's ear. He laughed. She tried to pull away, but he pulled her down onto his lap and started to kiss her. And then they were making out again in front of us.

"Jesus!" I said, no longer able to contain myself. "Get a fucking room!"

Freddie stood, still holding Kim. "*Pas de problème.*" And he carried her like that, all the way up the stairs.

Gregory and I woke in the middle of the night to Freddie and Kim moaning theatrically in the bathroom.

"Are they taking a shower?" Gregory whispered.

"They're going to wake the baby."

I became very aware of our two bodies on the futon—we still slept on the floor like undergrads—and I felt comforted by the usualness of it.

Gregory said, "What a strange night."

The shower stopped, the bathroom door creaked open, and we heard naked feet padding down the hallway to the guestroom.

Gregory turned on his side, his breath hot on my shoulder. I could feel him needing me, waiting for me to speak.

"Do you think we've let things slide?" he whispered. I thought he might be crying.

Finally, I rolled over and touched his damp cheek. Once I had liked his face a great deal. Once, I had chosen Gregory, and he had chosen me, and it was hard now to understand what we'd thought we were deciding—or if we were aware that we were making a life-shaping decision at all. When anything in the world felt possible, one decision here and there never seemed like it could lead to a future in which we were unhappy.

I kissed Gregory, and he kissed me back. "We'll be okay," I said. I could live with okay, I thought. "What does Freddie know?"

By the time I woke and fed Naomi, Gregory had eaten breakfast and gone back to sleep, Freddie was out jogging, and Kim was sunbathing topless on a blanket in the backyard.

"You might want to put something on," I suggested.

She sat up on her elbows and looked around. We were surrounded by tall grasses and trees. In the summer, the leaves created a veil between our yard and Grace and Jerry's white split-level.

"Who's going to see me?" Kim said, finally.

I gave up and put Naomi down on the blanket. "I brought you some blueberries. We picked them last week."

"Charming," she said and took the bowl from me.

I waited for her to say something about the night before, but she talked about her wedding instead.

"It's going to be easy-going. We want it to mean something. So we're asking a few close friends to speak at the reception, a poem or something? You always had a way with words."

I didn't think you had to ask your friends to toast you at your wedding. "You got it," I said.

She fed herself a handful of berries. It was a bright day, and maple-leaf shadows dappled her bare calves, spreading up and across her legs as a breeze blew in. Kim nodded, but she looked miserable. I couldn't believe I hadn't understood it before: the guarded way she'd been looking at me—or not looking at me at all.

I didn't know if she wanted me to notice or not, so I just asked, "Are you happy, Kim?"

Freddie came jogging up the driveway then, shirtless, drenched in sweat. He waved cheerily as he walked toward us.

"I understand what it must look like," Kim said. She paused, watching Freddie approach. "But I know what I'm getting into." She reached across the blanket and squeezed my hand. At her touch, the old happiness hovered between us, the old relief. "I was such a wreck in college, Mir. Being here brought all that back." She laughed. "You know? The bad old days."

For a moment, I couldn't get my bearings. "The bad old days," I repeated.

"But look at us now!"

I tried to laugh, too, but my mind was elsewhere, going over all my previous conversations with Kim and filtering them through this strange, new lens.

Freddie spotted Naomi then, and he called out, "How's my little princess?"

She crawled so fast, all of her limbs in sync. I wished Gregory were out here with us. When she reached his feet, Freddie smiled down at her, and she latched onto his leg and pulled herself into a standing position.

Freddie picked Naomi up and sat next to us. "*Bonjour,*" he said, admiring the sunshine with his upturned face.

I'd had just about enough of his middle-school French. "Good morning," I said, stressing every syllable.

Resting his free hand on Kim's shoulder blade, he gazed down at her admiringly. "I can't wait to breed with you."

"You'll be elderly by the time our kids can drive."

I half-smiled: it sounded like something the old Kim would say to get a laugh.

Freddie looked hurt for a moment. He took his hand off Kim's back and lifted Naomi up to the sky, making airplane sounds. "*Bien sur,*" he said. "I'll make an excellent elderly parent."

Naomi took her first step after breakfast.

Somehow Freddie had managed to get the projector

working, and we were gathered again in the living room, the heavy drapes shut and musty. Glasses remained scattered on the coffee table—more glasses than there had been drinkers. As we began the slideshow, Naomi bounced on my lap, and we toured every room of Kim and Freddie's home, an entire townhouse, right downtown. Every room was in the process of being renovated to make space for Kim's taste. She had her own studio, too, and I looked with admiration as Freddie clicked through slides of a new series of self portraits: Kim naked in front of her easel, eating a piece of birthday cake; Kim naked on a starkly lit stage, her mouth open in song while gazing out at an audience wearing their opera-finest; Kim naked in a museum gallery full of clothed and disinterested art patrons.

Mid-presentation, Naomi slipped off my lap and stood by herself on the worn carpet. Freddie stopped clicking through the slides, and there was only the hum of the projector and Naomi's quiet breathing. In the middle of the room, she turned her head, scoping us all out, our faces of surprise and delight.

In a few months, at Kim and Freddie's wedding reception, Naomi would be strong enough to toddle around the dance floor, greeting guests by grasping onto their pant legs and nylons. As she roamed about, charming people, I would take the microphone to tell everyone how Kim and I had once decorated every wall of our apartment with mirrors from Goodwill, many of which had fallen during a surprising earthquake. Not a single one of them had broken. "To good fortune and good friends," I would say, raising my glass to the beaming couple. Secretly, Gregory and I thought their marriage wouldn't last long, and I'm not proud to say we felt superior for thinking it, but four years later, as we greeted our son, Kim and Freddie were renewing their vows in Bermuda. "The light's wonderful," Kim wrote. "You'd be able to describe it better than me."

As we watched the slide show, Kim sat on the edge of her seat, cheering on my daughter. Freddie motioned at Naomi to walk to him. Gregory was on the floor now—kneeling, leaning forward. His face caught in a shaft of light from the projector, his head haloed by glowing dust particles. He smiled. Everyone could see what he saw: of all of us, Naomi had chosen him.

"You're walking!" Gregory cheered, genuinely thrilled. When he reached out his hand, our daughter toddled right into his arms, laughing as he caught her.

PORTS OF CALL

We don't arrive until dark. By the time Robert and I climb out of the car, sticky from a long day driving in the summer heat, my mother is waiting on the porch. Inside, my father plays an unfamiliar tune on the piano. Usually he would be in bed by now.

While Robert fetches the bags from the trunk, I carry my daughter toward the house, aware of something unsettled in my mother's narrowed shape. I try to put Lily down, but she grasps the collar of my shirt.

"He's been agitated," my mother says. "I might know why." She's about to explain, but then the music stops. When the screen door opens, Lily buries her face in my neck.

My father steps under the orange glow of the porch light, and under it, his skin appears thin and yellowed, like parchment, easily torn. His eyes skip from me to Lily.

Robert appears with our suitcases and a warm greeting.

Hesitant, my father takes my husband's extended hand without recognizing the man attached to it.

Since a car accident sixteen years ago, my father has been unable to remember anything for more than a matter of hours. Right now his gaze is inscrutable, but I think he knows me when he settles on my face in a familiar, wary stare. "Say hello to your grandfather," I coax. Lily gives him a shy wave, and my father places a heavy hand on her head, as if she were the neighbor's sturdy Labrador Retriever.

"We've come to celebrate your birthday, Dad!" I say, absurdly cheerful. Birthdays make no difference to him anymore, but my mother always insists we gather for these occasions.

His eyes turn stony. "Don't think for a minute that I don't realize I am a broken down old man." Slowly, angrily, he backs away from us, sending my mother a final, reproachful look.

He is often confused, sometimes grouchy, but never nihilistic. The screen door bangs shut behind him. In mute despair, I watch him stomp through the kitchen to the stairs.

My mother shrugs helplessly. "Maybe tomorrow," she says, but she hardly sounds convinced.

By tomorrow he will be surprised to see us all over again.

At the time of the accident, I was a sophomore with middling grades and no interests aside from boys. I had quit piano lessons and ballet years earlier. My apathy toward "self-improvement" drove my father crazy. So when I joined the drama club for a senior who got every lead in the school plays, my father, ever hopeful, saw an opportunity. For my birthday several months before the accident, he gave me a heavy, leather-bound copy of *The Collected Works of Shakespeare*. I rolled my eyes but accepted the book without complaint, because my senior was mad for Macbeth. I even learned a few lines—"Tomorrow, tomorrow, tomorrow"—which I used to good effect while taking off my clothes behind the painted forest from a production of *Once Upon a Mattress*. But mostly I just used Shakespeare to prop open my bedroom window, so I didn't have to leave the house at night to smoke.

Driving home one night from his job at his law firm downtown, my father's car was hit by a driver who ran through a stop sign. When he woke from the coma, he could not remember the accident or many events prior to it. *The Collected Works* and my stint with the theater were wiped from his memory.

After we tuck Lily into my old bed and after my mother makes sure my father is asleep and breathing evenly, the three of us gather on the front porch. There is a cool breeze off the lake tonight, and it is interludes like these—deceptively peaceful gatherings—when I feel my father's loss more than usual.

"Is he having a poor reaction to his meds?" I ask. "Seizures? Did the aid quit?"

My mother shakes her head. "I'm in love," she says, easing out the words, so there's no mistaking them. "And I think your father suspects." She smiles at my surprise, a bashful grin. "Try to keep an open mind," she urges. "I might not be a saint, but Terry has kept me sane over the years."

I admit it's not what I was expecting.

I knew Terry as a pale and earnest graduate student. A year after the accident, my father announced he was going to learn the piano, because "we couldn't let a good instrument go to waste." (A dig at me.) Terry needed the money. And my father's progress was truly an enigmatic triumph of memory. Every night while I pretended to do homework in my room, my father practiced his scales, and though new places and new and changing faces did not stick with him, notes did, building upon each other day after day to become layered constellations of remembered things. He was playing Haydn by the time I left for college.

My mother is looking at me, waiting for my response—my approval.

I want Robert to say something; his reaction will help me respond more appropriately. He sees me looking at him and turns his calm face to my mother. "I imagine it must be a relief to be with someone who can grow with you."

My mother nods appreciatively.

I say, "I don't know how you can do this to Dad."

At this, my mother begins to cry. "Terry and I can eat out and talk about the food after. He really loves to eat."

It's true that my father developed an extremely limited palate after the accident—chicken and rice for almost every meal—but it hardly seems the point.

"We're very discreet," she offers, wiping her tears with the sleeve of her light sweater. "Your father couldn't possibly know. But he's been asking if there's someone else."

After a long silence, during which we all look awkwardly at each other, my mother seems to rouse herself. "Whatever you think, Elizabeth, Terry really loves your father. They get along so well. It doesn't matter that he has to reintroduce himself every week."

She stands, and I expect her to say goodnight, but instead she has more awkward news: "He's coming over tomorrow. To, you know, celebrate."

"I can't think of a worse idea."

Upstairs in the study, I sit on the edge of the futon, flipping through my father's photo album from 1996. Years ago he mapped his strange new world through roll upon roll of Polaroid film and hours of videotape. He still keeps stacks of these notated albums and boxes of now-obsolete VHS tapes on the shelves here, but he prefers writing these days; a small notebook can travel with him in his back pocket, and if he forgets about it, he can sit without breaking it. In this album are Polaroids from our camping trip to Glacier National Park, when he went off on a trail by himself, got lost, and made it back to our site by retracing his steps through pictures of the trail.

Robert sits down next to me, moves the album back to its place on the shelf, and pulls me to him.

"I suppose that living with an amnesiac inures one to certain strangenesses," he says.

I nod against his chest. But I don't feel at all inured. Instead, I've become more keenly aware of my strangenesses. I flirt with men I don't know. I'm pathologically nervous about flying. I often speak harshly to the people I love. I feel each of these flaws as its own weight, a burden I hope not to pass along to my child.

I push away from Robert to look at him. "You're so good," I say.

"And it's exhausting, let me tell you." He is both joking and not joking. Just this morning, as we were leaving the house, I was yelling at him about some stupid thing. About the cooler. Lily was already wailing in her car seat when I realized Robert hadn't packed the cooler with ice and sandwiches. Or, neither of us had, but I decided it was his fault.

He starts taking off his clothes for bed. Watching his beautiful and familiar body, I don't know what I would do if tomorrow morning he could not remember me. As I lean against him, he helps me lift my sticky shirt above my head. He kisses my neck and eyelids, and this is how I know we're good, that tomorrow we will be, too.

I wake at nine feeling unrested. Rather than go downstairs, I lie in bed until Lily pounces, her grandfather's present in her hands. The wrapping paper is plain brown, like a grocery bag, and she has drawn purple fish on the outside to make the gift look festive. "Now," she says, tugging on my arm with unexpected force. Gone is the timid, limp girl from last night.

Robert is already in the kitchen, making coffee, chatting with my father, who surprises me with a pleasant smile. "Your man here has just been telling me about this porch he's building."

"Oh, yes, the deck. Robert is very handy."

I raise my eyebrows at my husband: No mention of the affair? No morning cynicism? Robert shakes his head no.

Lily holds the package out to my father. "It's your birthday," she says.

"Sweet child," he says. "Help me unwrap this."

Lily approves of this suggestion, and once her decorated

paper is destroyed, she holds up a hooded sweatshirt for my father to see—across the front in blue letters is the name of the college where Robert and I teach.

"Good school," my father says.

Every year Robert and I wrack our brains: what does one get for an amnesiac? Sometimes we joke that we should just take back the present after my father has unwrapped it, then rewrap it the next year. Surprise! Just what you always wanted!

"It's perfect," my father says. He looks at me and smiles. "Because it's still chilly out and my daughter and I are going for a little paddle."

I haven't been in the canoe with my father since I was an unwilling teenage passenger, grumbling about having to wear a life preserver. I'm still in my sweatpants and a t-shirt, and I say I will change.

"Nonsense," my father says. "We'll go directly. Take a jacket from the hall closet." He tosses me a banana. "Sustenance."

Robert mouths "Go."

In the canoe, my father tells me to head across the lake, where he and Mom birdwatch. We paddle silently for a good ten minutes. I don't know how I've gotten myself into the back of the canoe. I have no idea how to steer.

My father clears his throat in a concerned, fatherly way, and I expect the worst. "This Robert of yours. Good guy. Smarter than the boys you usually bring home. We had a good talk about his interest in nineteenth-century theater."

Poor Robert. Always the new guy. After my father's accident, my boyfriends were fascinated with—and liberated by—the idea that he could not remember them, no matter how many times I brought them home with me. But for Robert, this peculiarity is merely the thing about my family he has to grapple with every visit, the way other spouses might have to deal with a highly critical-in-law.

"Robert's very well-regarded in his field." I say it even though it will soon mean nothing out here in the boat.

My father's strokes are weak, leaving me to do the bulk of the paddling. We're close to the other side when my father points to a spot ahead, and somehow I get us there and keep us from drifting. This is a private cove—no houses or swimmers. Far away, on the side of the lake we just came from, a group of kayakers speed close to the shore.

"Good place to see some Spotted Sandpipers." He reaches for the binoculars around his neck and peers through them. "Sometimes a Loon or two. Good god, look at that magnificent Cardinal!" He pulls out his journal from his back pocket and flips through it to make a notation—the place, the bird—and then he stops, looking down at a page I cannot see. I hear him muttering, but I cannot make out what he's saying.

"Everything okay, Dad?"

He turns to me, shaking the boat a little. "I think your mother is seeing someone."

I shake my head, not meeting his gaze. "What are you talking about?"

"Look." He holds out the journal.

I take the small book and scan backwards through my father's crisp handwriting and bulleted notations:

- *Morning. In canoe with Bethy: distant, hard to figure out.*
- *Saw: Cardinal.*
- *Bethy arrives today, Joan says. Joan agitated and impatient.*

And then I see the culprit:

- *Came inside from reading newspaper, heard Joan on the phone upstairs, picked up downstairs line—don't know why, very rude—and heard her say "I love you," to a man. I did not know his voice.*

Dad's back is to me now. I take a deep breath. "Maybe it's not what you think," I say, prepared to regurgitate the clichéd script from every film I've ever seen about adultery.

"What's not what I think?"

"Maybe Mom isn't—"

But he's distracted, looking through his binoculars again,

and he lowers them to begin patting the big front pocket of his sweatshirt, and then all the pockets of his trousers. "I thought I brought my journal with me," he says. "To write all this down for posterity."

I glance at the small book in my hand, and it's so easy I don't even hate myself for it: I slip it into the inside of the windbreaker I grabbed from the closet. Although I can't quite believe this will work, I'm not sure what else to do. I tell myself that my mother *does* deserve to love someone who remembers the meals they ate together and the words they spoke the night before. And I tell myself that my father deserves not to know.

"I guess you can tell I'm a little off today," he says.

"You seem fine. Fit as a fiddle."

"You can humor me all you like, kid-o. But I'm a broken down old man."

This time, there is no bitterness, only resignation.

Eventually, he stops looking for the journal and starts paddling again, this time away from the cove, back toward the middle of the lake. "What did you say your boyfriend does?" He pulls up the hood of the sweatshirt he received this morning.

"He's a Professor, Dad. We both teach in the theater department."

"Theater might be a good fit for you, Miss Drama Queen. You really should develop some hobbies."

I laugh, but I'm not feeling very up to the act this morning. For a couple of years after the accident, I put on a regular show for my father; I kept my volume of Shakespeare on the coffee table and would try to be seen reading from it when he was around. I could quote all sorts of lines, from all different plays, but my father never remembered giving me that book, and though he would praise me for memorizing such weighty lines, within a few hours he would forget I'd ever learned them. My senior year of college, my mother took him to see me as Rosalind in *As You Like It*, and she said he watched the entire play with his mouth open, disbelieving and in tears.

By the time we reach our dock, it must be close to noon, and both our noses have turned pink from the sun.

Robert reads on the porch. When he looks up from his book, I pat my breast pocket. "I stole his journal," I whisper. "I'm a terrible person."

In the kitchen, I find my mother standing in front of the open freezer. "I forgot what I was looking for." Her eyes are tired and puffy. "Ice cream. Of course. Terry will be here soon."

For a second I want to yell at her. Fuck the ice cream! Why bother with these silly pretenses when my father wouldn't know the difference? But I watch my mother hand Lily candles, one by one; I watch my father come in, shouting, "A beautiful cake—what's the occasion?" And I understand why we bother.

Terry looks taller than I remember and awkwardly cheerful, carrying a giant bowl of fruit salad. He greets Robert, hugs me, tells me I look well, admires Lily's outfit—which pleases her immensely—and shakes my father's hand. My father appears bemused and pleased by Terry's arrival. They are strangely like old friends, although my father does not know his name. My mother makes a quick explanation: "John, this is Terry, your piano teacher. He's come to help celebrate your birthday. You know Terry."

"I believe I do," my father says, confused, looking at my mother for reassurance.

She nods at him, smiles at Terry once, but otherwise keeps busy gathering plates and coffee cups.

I follow her into the dining room with a handful of spoons. From across the table, I catch her eye. "So much for being discreet," I whisper. "He heard you two on the phone and wrote it down in his journal."

She looks horrified.

"I have the journal," I say. I want her to tell me what to do with it.

"Okay," she says, clearly relieved. "Okay."

We sing a tentative version of "Happy Birthday" around the dining room table. With Lily's assistance, my father blows out the ten candles on his cake, and Terry cheers. He looks at my mother a lot, and I am glad to see it is an adoring look, but not obviously lustful. The mood here is almost light, just this side of festive, so we are surprised when my father turns serious and brooding behind a forkful of cake.

"I have some things to say," he says. "An important thing you should all know." He gazes at my mother, and I wonder for a second if it is not the journal at all; maybe my father just *knows*, in his gut—or the part of his brain that remembers music—that my mother and Terry are in love. And seeing them next to each other and hearing Terry's voice has triggered the memory.

Clearly, my mother has the same thought. "Shit," she whispers, and Terry takes her hand under the table. I try to catch his eye to tell him not to, but he will not look my way.

My father seems to notice none of this. "I have to say thank you, thank you for being here." Then, out of nowhere, he laughs, a big and rich laugh I haven't heard since I was a child. "I didn't even know it was my birthday!"

My newly jolly father sends more slices around the table, more cake than we have people, and everyone laughs, everyone teases him, and he doesn't seem to mind.

I'm so distracted by the mirth that I can't eat.

"Your cake is getting cold," my father says. A little wink at Lily, who winks back.

"Take me out in the canoe," she says. "Show me your favorite places."

I look at Robert.

But it turns out we don't have to decide how to tell them no, because the question has reminded my father about boats in general, and then he's talking up the beautiful wooden boats he used to work on up in Maine as a college student. These boats, in turn, remind him of being an officer in the Navy. Animated, he describes his three years on the USS Princeton during the Vietnam War, and we all listen, rapt but nervous in the presence of his vigorous memory. "We had everything we needed on that ship, it was like a little city unto itself. But I tell you I longed for those ports of call." Pushing away from the table quickly, he knocks over a pitcher of milk my mother brought out for our coffees, and bounds upstairs, leaving all of us to stare at each other.

After a few minutes, he returns with a curious prize: a matchbook that he drops in my hand. A bar or restaurant's faded address is written in pretty Japanese script beneath a woodcut of a snow-capped mountain. "I had a whole collection of these at one time," he says. "All the signs in Tokyo were in Japanese, of course, so I'd show these matchbooks to a driver or a man on the street. The only way I could find my way around."

He is oblivious to Terry's hand on my mother's back now. Robert watches my father with his usual, polite curiosity, and Lily has a fistful of cake moving toward her mouth. I do not bother reminding her about table manners.

My father explains that whether coming to shore or leaving it, his post was always in the boiler room, always inside the ship. Out at sea for seven months at a time, he never saw the shore as the ship approached or departed. "I imagine that was the most beautiful thing," he says, "watching the earth appear on the horizon."

He has left all his frosting, and now he hands his plate to Lily. With relish, she bends her face to lick the extra bit of chocolate. Finally, I have the mind to tell her no, and she looks at me with displeasure.

"You look just like Bethy," my father says to Lily. "When Bethy was your age."

Lily says nothing; her little hands grasp the plate.

"When Bethy was a little older than you, she blossomed into a very difficult child."

"I'm not difficult."

He looks at Robert, then me. "I hope her parents have started her on an instrument."

Robert puts his arm around my shoulders. "We thought we'd let her decide what she likes."

"I want to play the tambourine."

"That's a start." My father ruffles Lily's hair, then stands from the table and points very suddenly and rudely at Terry.

"What about you," my father says.

"What about me?" Terry tries on a calm smile.

I wait, unsettled by my own pleasurable expectation. He does know.

But then he shrugs, bewildered by his own demands. "You play an instrument?"

Patiently, my mother says, "Terry plays the piano, John. He's your piano teacher."

My father drops his pointing finger and his face relaxes. "Of course you are. So why don't you come teach me some notes?"

While my mother and I wash dishes in the kitchen, my father plays a Scarlatti sonata. My mother hums along with it. The minor chords remind me of going off to college and hoping I wouldn't have to return home.

"See?" my mother says. "Everything worked out."

I am not so sure, but I do not say so. She is the one who wakes up every morning with my father, she is the one who reminds him of what is important every day: exercise, medications, breakfast. And because she does not say how weird it is that in the other room, the two men she loves are playing the piano together, I do not mention it either.

As I dry and put away a plate, I look around the kitchen— the silver-flecked linoleum that has begun to peel up in the corners. My windbreaker hangs on a peg by the door, and tucked in its pocket is my father's journal—a year or more of memories. Everything smells like lake water. The piano notes fill the room, and underneath them is the rhythm of the refrigerator's motor, almost as old as me, humming along just fine.

SHELTER

Margaret

On Friday afternoon, while waiting for her father to arrive with his new girlfriend, Margaret tended to the rabbits in the shed with her mother's help. First she swept the hay and droppings from under Cindy Lauper's hutch. Then slowly, and with great tenderness in her heart, she filled Mr. T's water bottle and measured his grainy pellets with more precision than usual. Margaret hoped that by stretching out every task, she might slow time enough to stop it completely. As she worked, the rabbits peered expectantly from their cages. They looked nervous, breathing hard in the thick heat of August. Margaret had always loved the annual trip with her father to the races in Saratoga, but today she did not want to go. This year, she was ten-years-old.

It wasn't just the rabbits—Margaret didn't want to leave

her mother, either. Helen, however, went about the usual chores with a blushing joy.

Humming a light tune as she fed Mary Poppins a wedge of lettuce through the slats of her cage, Helen said, "I know it's probably hard. To see your father with someone else."

"Not really," Margaret said, too quiet for her mother to hear. How could she explain so that it didn't sound mean or false? The truth was, the girlfriend meant very little to Margaret. She seemed nice enough two weekends ago when they'd been introduced over hot-fudge sundaes at Friendly's. She hadn't spoken to Margaret in the chirpy voice most adults used with her. And Margaret supposed it must be nice for her father to have someone to talk to. His apartment still felt vacant, even though he'd lived there for over a year.

No, it was her mother's secret happiness that worried Margaret. Before, her mother had always grown sadder as a visiting weekend neared and Margaret packed her little blue suitcase to take to her father's apartment. Before, Margaret had felt the bond between her and her mother sharpen as she pulled away from the house in her father's rusty station wagon. Now Helen was practically floating, untethered from her daughter. Smiling to herself, she reached into the cage to scratch Mary Poppins's forehead, where the elderly rabbit liked to be touched most. It disturbed Margaret that her mother had plans she didn't want to share.

Even more disquieting: Margaret knew vaguely that the plans had to do with the neighbor, Cass. He was married to Nancy! But Margaret still knew. She'd watched him and her mother flirt at the Harringtons' barbeque last week. She'd heard her mother take recent, late-night calls, voice muffled but giddy. Last night, standing outside Helen's room with a glass of milk—she had trouble sleeping on hot nights—she'd heard a few words of the plan: "After her father...yes...Are you sure I won't fall in?...no...she's back Sunday evening."

It shocked Margaret how little adults thought she understood.

She had an uncanny ability to pick up on the emotional lives of the grownups around her, and the tensions and strange intimacies that grew between them over time. It wasn't just with Cass and her mother—she'd known well before her parents told her that they were going to divorce, and the announcement had actually come as some relief after ages of coolness and sharp words between them. She had always believed she and her mother were a sufficient pair; her father was a nice but busy man, always traveling for work, and they didn't really need him in the day-to-day workings of family. So when he left, very little changed for Margaret, except that things got better.

Now things seemed on the verge of getting worse. Complicated. Cass demanded too much from people—he always wanted to know how you were doing, what your hobbies were, what television shows and music you enjoyed. Margaret didn't see why anyone needed to know those things, unless they were your friends. Then there was Cass's toddler, Ross, a constant screamer, and Margaret feared and envied his daughter Riley, a pretty and sullen thirteen-year-old whose own rabbits often took home blue ribbons from the 4H fairs. Would Riley become her sister now? And what would happen to Nancy, the chain smoker? She had always given Margaret an extra scoop of chocolate at the town's ice cream socials, and Margaret liked her steady, pleasant smile; she always seemed apart from other people, but not sad about it, and Margaret could relate to this way of being in the world.

She reached into Mr. T's cage to pat his long, black fur while he cowered in the corner. He was her first angora, the one she loved most, even though he'd never won a thing. When she was younger and considering becoming a vegan, she'd asked her mother if Mr. T would be happier in the woods behind their house, with the wild rabbits she sometimes saw there, and her mother had laughed gently. "He wouldn't last a minute."

Helen was staring into Miss Pretty's hutch, the special hutch that Cass had made out of cedar.

"Look how sweet, Margaret."

Margaret didn't want to look at Miss Pretty's kits: helpless little things—hairless and blind. Miss Pretty was supposed to be her rabbit, a gift. When Riley's tawny angora had had a litter, Cass brought one of them to Margaret, but Margaret knew Miss Pretty was really intended for her mother.

Just then, Helen straightened. "They're here," she said. She looked at her daughter finally, radiant with expectation, and Margaret thought she was the most beautiful woman in the world. "Shall we bring them in to see the bunnies?"

Margaret wanted to cry. "No."

In that moment, for once, she wanted to be childish. Shoving Mr. T back into his hutch without ceremony, she forgot to kiss his nose in her customary good-bye to him. And then she bolted from the barn, toward her father's waiting car and her little blue suitcase, packed and ready on the porch steps.

Alice

They stood at the white fence to watch the horses and their jockeys and trainers parade past, toward the paddock. Post Time—a phrase Alice had only just learned—was at 1pm. It was now 11:30 on Saturday, and they had already breakfasted at the Clubhouse and taken a tour of the place where all the horses lived during their weeks at Saratoga. The stables, the Backstretch. Where the horses, slick from their morning workouts, mechanically ate the hay from the baskets in front of their stalls.

Alice didn't want to complain, but she felt overheated and confused by the pageantry: the sea of people—some of them in ridiculous hats—the smell of dirt and hay, and a sense of anticipation that she found inexplicable but encompassing, as if she were in church again and listening to pretty but strange hymns. In the midst of it, Henry was trying to coach Margaret on this year's crop—did you call it a crop of horses? Alice tuned out and let herself be lulled by the delighted murmurs of people who knew better. It was Henry who had insisted she come along this weekend; he wanted Margaret to get comfortable around them as a couple before they told her they were moving in together.

Alice thought it was probably too early and not the right venue; her instincts suggested trouble ahead. But now that she was here, she wanted Margaret to like her, and she wanted Henry to be proud of her for winning over his daughter without being obsequious. She'd had success with children in the past—her niece and nephew, her best friend's toddler. But they were all soft and easy to please. She could make silly faces, and they would laugh.

Silly faces would not fly with Margaret. Right now Alice was dying to know what the girl was thinking, what she thought of her, whether or not she resented Alice's presence. Fleetingly, she conjured the image of Helen, standing tall in her driveway yesterday with a thick, tan rabbit in her arms. Poised and gracious, with a stirring light behind her eyes, she seemed immediately like someone Alice would want to know more, if circumstances were different. It made her sad to think about, so she did not think about Helen for long.

For her part, Margaret was intent on her project: studying each horse as it went by, matching it with the names in her program, which she'd had signed by several jockeys already that morning.

"Point out your favorites," Alice requested mildly.

The girl obliged without taking her eyes off the horses: "That one giving his trainer some trouble was Greek Revival. Dad says he's spirited, but unpredictable. Here's Sheer Perfection. I'd go for her, but the jockey's a novice." She made a notation in her program as a velvety brown horse neared. "DoubleHappiness." She nodded decidedly. "That one's mine."

Henry leaned back from the fence and raised his eyebrows at Alice, as if they were in on it together. "A long shot, kiddo. Check out that wobble on his back leg."

"I don't care."

Alice saw an opportunity. "I like his name," she agreed.

Margaret flicked her cool, green eyes over Alice once, then looked away. "Yes, you have to like the name, I think." She didn't smile.

Such a serious child, a girl with no nickname: "Not Meg, or Maggie or Marge," Henry had advised. "She hates all those." Even he found her to be difficult to know—so wary and distant. Only at ease around her rabbits and other animals. Last night she'd barely spoken to them but had spent hours in the hot hotel pool, swimming—back and forth, back and forth—apparently oblivious to the knot of children playing Marco Polo with gusto around her.

"Do we place our bets now?" Alice asked. "You'll need to show me how, Margaret."

Margaret eyed Alice wearily. "Dad places the bets. I'm underage."

"But you know the ropes," Henry said. He rubbed Alice's shoulder gently.

Margaret shrugged and started walking. She appeared to be leading them, and they followed wordlessly, instinctively. Over her shoulder, she called to Alice, "Don't listen to my dad. Our horse is a winner."

Our horse. Alice smiled and squeezed Henry's hand.

Her lease was up at the end of the month, then she would move into his big, empty place. She had ideas about furniture, about how to make a room inviting.

"It's show time," Henry said.

She felt a little hopeful.

Riley

Riley hated her parents, even though she was vaguely aware that she had loved them intensely when she was younger. The pictures were still on the fridge to remind her: sweet depictions of grinning stick families on their way to the zoo or the park. But her mother and father were useless to her now, wrapped up as they were in their own selfish pursuits and sticking her with this little shit of a brother for all of Saturday afternoon.

She couldn't get him to shut up. He wanted another ice cream sandwich for lunch, and even though he wasn't supposed to have even one, she gave him a second. He was a slow eater, so the process kept him occupied, if hiccupping back small sobs, and her desire for the momentary quiet trumped her feeling of disgust at the mess he was making of himself. After he finished, fingers caked in vanilla ice cream and chocolate, she suggested he go wash his hands. But first she let him wipe them on her mother's white linen tablecloth. Back and forth, back and forth, grinning warily.

"Happy now?"

"Yes," he whispered. But his eyes still glistened with tears.

His sudden timidity annoyed her. "Now what do we do?" she snapped, consumed with helpless anger.

He started to cry again.

"No, please don't. Oh, please, don't cry anymore."

She went to pick him up and apologize, but he was slick with sweat, and when she grasped at him, he wriggled easily out of her fingers, slid from his chair, and ran past her. Before she could reach him again, he was out the back door and running into the yard.

She followed, blaming her mother with every step. Nancy was supposed to be here, taking care of Ross while their father was in Maine for two days, his yearly trip to visit a buddy from college. He always returned with crates of sluggish lobsters for the Labor Day Weekend lobster bake they hosted in the backyard; it was the final hurrah before school started again.

And today was supposed to be her special celebration—the afternoon pool party and evening bonfire over at the Lingates' farm. The rumors had been promising: that Jason Miller would be there, that he had finally broken up with Susie Bennett, and that he had asked a couple of people if Riley might show up.

But her mother had invented some emergency with her sister down the road, a woman who was always in trouble. Divorcing her husband, sobbing in their kitchen about car payments—it just wasn't how an adult should behave. Anyway, her mother had gone, of course. Who knew when she'd be back? Riley believed she worried more about Rina than she did about her own children.

Riley was exhausted from running, and when Ross finally tripped over a divot in the grass, she was able to catch him. He slapped at her face with his dirty fingers.

"That's it," she said. "You're getting it now." She hauled him, screaming, to the hose next to the rabbit hutches. Holding him with one hand, she turned on the tap, set Ross down, and sprayed him. He screeched and ran from her. But he came back, grinning.

"More," he demanded.

She rolled her eyes. Of course he would like the punishment she'd designed for him. When he was happy, he looked like their father.

Once they were both soaking wet, laughing—even Riley, in spite of herself—they checked in on the rabbits and refilled their water bottles because it was so hot.

Inside the house, it would be even hotter, so even though it was time for Ross's nap, Riley took him for a walk through the woods behind the house, down to the creek, and let him wade in it, looking for tadpoles.

Soon, though, he grew cranky again and started to kick at the water. If he got hurt on the rocks, it would definitely be her fault, and she didn't need one more thing to worry about. "You want to see the babies?" she asked.

Ross nodded.

Margaret's kits. Riley felt they almost belonged to her. It still made her mad to think about how quickly her father had given away Miss Pretty. Even Ross loved her tiny babies, though he was not allowed to touch them. Helen had said they could visit whenever they wanted; the shed was always open. So she picked up her brother, and they headed toward the neighbors', following the creek down to where the fallen tree made a bridge from their side to the darker part of the woods. On the other side, the trees were older and denser. They stretched a ways, ending at an abandoned gravel pit where Riley and her friends used to play tag on the mounds of stone.

It was dark enough here that Riley could imagine what the night would feel like, holding Jason's hand beside the fire. Her friends said he was fast, but that didn't bother her. She could take care of herself; she knew what she wanted. In her arms, Ross felt heavier. She looked down at his face and saw that he was asleep, and she almost stopped resenting him then, he'd gone so sweet and peaceful. But then she remembered she'd have to walk home like this; once he fell asleep, he was a goner, and if she tried putting him down to walk, the screaming would be impossible.

Just as they were starting to turn around, she heard footsteps on dry leaves. Scrambling as best as she could to get away from the creek's edge and behind a tree, she felt her pulse in her throat, imagining a dangerous encounter in which she would play either the blameless victim or the hero who saved her brother's life. There used to be stories about creeps hanging out at the gravel pit, just waiting to kidnap the children who played there.

Two people emerged from the denser trees, making their way toward the creek. It took her a moment to understand. A girl didn't expect her father to be in the woods, this was her terrain. Besides, he wasn't supposed to be anywhere but in Maine. He had left in the middle of the night as he always did, so he could drive in the dark with the windows open and be one of the few cars on the road. He wasn't supposed to be back until Sunday night, after dinner. But here he was, carrying a bag that was not his own—she could tell even from this distance—and that the person with him was Helen. Her long, dark hair was pulled back in its usual bun. Years ago, she had taught Riley's beginning tap class. Sometimes she would hug Riley in front of the other girls, as if they were best friends, or family. It had always embarrassed her, and she'd been relieved when her mother told her she could quit.

Riley couldn't make sense of what she was seeing, but she felt dizzy, sick to her stomach. It was like watching a horror movie. It brought back the sound of tap shoes in the studio.

"You don't need to help," Helen said, angrily. "I've got it this time."

They were far away, but voices traveled further in summer; they gathered weight and density. Her father tried to hold Helen's hand, but she grabbed for her knapsack, which she threw on her back like an awkward school-kid, and began scrambling across the log on her hands and knees.

On the other side, Riley's father remained still, arms hanging. "I'm sorry. Helen, I'm sorry." He did not go after her, and Helen did not look back but steamed ahead and up the bank toward her own backyard.

Ross still had not stirred.

Once her father disappeared from sight, Riley began to jog. Ross only started to wake up as she reached the house. She could see her mother's car in the driveway, but her father's truck still hadn't appeared.

She found Nancy smoking on the back deck. As Riley climbed the steps, Nancy tapped her matchbook against the porch railing, then left it there. She walked over and stroked Riley's long hair.

"You take him out for a little stroll?" Her voice sounded uneven, like she'd been crying, but her gaze was firm and dry.

"By the creek. I can put him to bed." She started to pull away, to go inside with her brother, but she felt she should say something more. "Aunt Rina okay?"

Nancy paused before speaking. "She had some news that concerned me."

Something shifted inside Riley, an instinct. "About Dad?"

She waited for her mother to respond, but Nancy just stood, flicked her cigarette into the yard, and took Ross from his sister. He snuggled into her shoulder. "You want me to drive you to that party, baby?" She leaned in to kiss Riley's head.

Riley was surprised to realize she didn't want to go anywhere right now. "I want to stay with you," she said. Her mother would take care of everything; she always did. Riley had forgotten what it felt like to want shelter like this. What it felt like to find it right in front of you.

But hugging her mother for the first time in months, taking in her smell of deodorant and tobacco, she began to feel protective and angry. She, too, could take care of some things. She could navigate the rabbit shed in the dark; she didn't need to turn on a light to know Miss Pretty's cage. She would wait until the sun set. Maybe her father would be home by then, and he would realize what she knew.

"I'll stay with you," she repeated. She wiped away her tears before Nancy could see them.

Helen

They began as planned: at the fallen tree, at 2am. Cass waited there with a flashlight. He turned it off to embrace her, and his arms wrapped awkwardly around her stuffed backpack. She had not been able to figure out what to take on an illicit weekend in Maine, so she packed too much and ended up feeling silly, not alluring.

After all this anticipation, she couldn't think of anything to say. Holding Cass, finally, she felt nervous. They'd known each other for years, but the flirting was relatively new, since her divorce. She realized that being alone made her more susceptible to loneliness, but she also truly cared for Cass. They had not yet slept together.

"Ready?" he said. She heard doubt in his voice, too.

But gently, he took her hand and led her across the tree. After weeks without rain, it was no longer slick with moss. The creek was lower than usual. In the halo of Cass's flashlight, the boulders looked sharp above the water's edge.

His truck was parked in the gravel pit, behind the one small outbuilding that remained there. It did not feel like a romantic place, but coastal Maine seemed like a long way off. Once inside the truck cab, she kissed him again, then brought his warm, calloused hands up under her shirt.

Groaning, he pulled her onto his lap and clutched her hungrily. She felt beautiful, expansive, connected. But when she began tugging at his belt buckle, he turned his head one way, then the other, as if they were being watched.

She laughed and kissed him again. "Just us and the foxes."

Gazing over her shoulder across the dashboard, he said, "Riley used to play here. I never thought it was a nice place for kids."

She slid off his lap reluctantly. "I get it. Not exactly sunset point." But that wasn't what he was saying, she knew. It wasn't the lack of pretty scenery, it was what the scenery made him think of: his children. Nancy.

She clicked her seat belt on, rebuffed and confused. And for the first time, a little guilty. Joining Cass for the weekend had been her bold suggestion, but he had accepted the idea eagerly two weeks ago, then planned carefully how they would meet and leave town unseen by prying neighbors. He'd been the one making excuses for months to come over to see her: the moss-covered roof that Henry had neglected for years, Miss Pretty's hutch, Ross's eagerness to see the baby rabbits. Two weeks before, while Margaret was out meeting her father's new girlfriend—according to a mutual friend, an accomplished musician—Cass had stopped by with a basket of zucchini and tomatoes from Nancy's garden. "I love you, Helen Schwartz," he had declared while she filled her crisper drawer with fresh vegetables. Oh, how good it felt to hear that! "Take me with you to Bar Harbor," she'd replied before kissing him.

She said nothing and let Cass start the truck and pull out onto the quiet road that snaked up to the highway. Several miles outside of town, he pulled over at a gas station to buy condoms and a pack of cigarettes. When he came back, he drove off in a hurry, his hands visibly trembling.

"Fuck," he whispered. "Rina was in there, buying cough drops."

Helen was confused. "At this hour?"

"They put her on the nightshift at the hospital all this month."

Her pulse quickened, but she tried to be rational. "She couldn't have seen me. No one drove in while I was waiting."

Cass shrugged. "Yeah."

They drove up 88 to 90 and through Albany in near silence, except for the radio, tuned to an inane talk-radio station that Helen could have done without. One thing she had always appreciated about Henry: he enjoyed quiet on a long car ride. She found it ironic that she was driving the same stretch of road he, Margaret, and the new girlfriend had taken just this afternoon. Last August was the first summer she had not also gone to Saratoga with her husband and daughter. It didn't bother her. She hated the whole idea of horse racing, how the animals were used and used up, how the people who truly cared for them rarely received the recognition they deserved.

Somewhere on the Mass Pike, she was startled out of a light sleep by Cass's hand on her thigh. "You okay?" he asked.

He was a kind man, she truly believed that. He'd never said a bad word about Nancy. His wife was not the reason they were doing this. For the first time in her life, she thought maybe there was such a thing as destiny. She nodded. "You?"

He sighed, apparently from relief. "I think I'm good."

Tentatively, he put his arm around her, and as his fingers tapped her bare shoulder, she became very aware of all the signs for motels they passed. The plan was to drive all the way through to Bar Harbor, where Cass had an old friend ("He won't mind") with a big house on the water. But now that they were on the road and out of the state, she did not see the need to wait. "Can we stop? I always used to like a good EconoLodge."

He took the next exit, and drove down the long, glowing strip of gas stations and fast food restaurants. It was early in the morning, a strange time to ask for a bed, but the motel receptionist blinked back sleep and handed them their room key.

Room 303 had no personality, of course, and the neutral ground presented a challenge: who were they outside their usual context—the houses and family and landscape that defined them? Inside, Helen and Cass grew awkward again, as if they were strangers.

They watched the weather channel for a while, their fingertips intertwined on top of the bedspread. Then Helen went into the bathroom to brush her teeth and put on her pretty, silk robe. When she came out again, Cass was naked under the sheets, crying. He looked up at her with an expression of pure anguish.

"I've never felt about anyone the way I feel about you, Helen."

She sat next to him and caressed his warm back. She let her robe fall open, because this was what they came for; she wanted him to see her.

"But this is a mistake," he said. "I got carried away."

Slowly, taking in her error, she drew back from him and tightened the robe around her waist. Perched on the edge of the double bed, her back straight, she could not look at him anymore. Her entire body still tingled from anticipation, but it was as if each nerve ending were being rubbed out, rubbed raw. She felt betrayed. By Cass. By her own desire.

"Take me home then."

As she gathered the few toiletries she'd removed from her bag, she told herself she should not be embarrassed, but she couldn't help feeling it. She'd yielded so easily to Cass's passionate declarations, and what had she gotten for her troubles? Tomorrow morning, she would still live next door to this man and his wife and children. Of course, that would have been true regardless of what happened here, but even though they'd never planned past this weekend, part of her had assumed they would get to that, or that it didn't matter, because being with him felt right.

They ate a tense and quiet breakfast at a diner, where the waitress seemed to take pity on them with deliberate cheer and heaping plates of home fries. After, they got right back on the road they'd just driven on.

In the end, Cass insisted on walking her back to the tree. She did not ask what he planned to do, whether he intended to go directly home, or how he would explain his early return, minus the lobsters. Maybe he would find lobsters somewhere else, or maybe he would confess everything to Nancy. Maybe tomorrow Helen would wake up a pariah in a town where she'd lived most of her adult life.

Back home, the house settled around her in its rambling vacancy—its rooms that hinted at a life once shared. The house was almost two hundred years old, and Helen felt both naïve and ancient standing alone in her bedroom. She missed Margaret.

When it grew dark, she called the hotel number Henry had left—even though it was late—and asked her former husband to put their daughter on the phone.

Margaret sounded sweet and cheerful. "Is it okay if I stay an extra day with Dad and Alice?"

Her heart dipped and swelled. "You're having a good time then?" She tried to sound happy.

"Our horse came in second. Alice likes underdogs, too."

While Margaret spoke, chattier than usual, Helen gazed through the window at their dark backyard. There was no moon tonight; the clouds had taken over the sky, and even though it hurt her to hear Margaret so entirely charmed, Helen kept her voice lilting, hopeful. Perhaps it might finally rain, she thought. Her blouse stuck to her skin. She hadn't put her bra back on after the motel. Thinking about it made her cringe, and when she opened her eyes, she noticed a flicker of light in the window of the rabbit shed. A flame, followed by sparks.

"I miss you," she called into the phone before dashing outside. "I miss you," she said again into the night. Under Miss Pretty's cage, a tiny fire was gathering strength in a pile of hay and newspaper. Quickly, and without thinking, she doused the flames with the hose out back.

Only when the flames went out did she have time to feel afraid, time to wonder who had set this cruel little fire and why they would do it. It would be about Cass, she was sure of it, but she could not imagine steady Nancy setting out to do physical harm. The fire had not been set long before—thank god she had seen it in time. She switched on the dim, overhead light.

"You poor things," she said loudly. If the person who had set the fire were nearby, they would be able to hear her, they would know she had the mind to act. "Poor babies," she cooed, going to open Miss Pretty's hutch, to take her out and soothe her.

But Miss Pretty was not inside. Helen could only see the kits—sleeping, almost motionless— tucked into the nest of fur and straw at the back.

She whirled around. Peering into one hutch after another, she saw that each was empty. She hunted longest for Mr. T, Margaret's favorite, who sometimes hid quite expertly. But he was definitely not inside, either.

Filled with panic, she ran outside. She could not think of whose name to call into the dark, or what to do next.

Her feet were bare. The grass felt dry and brittle. Less than 24 hours before, the woods in front of her had promised a more enchanted life. Even now, she could convince herself that the flickers of light in the dark were the eyes of her daughter's prize-winning rabbits. Although skittish and overwhelmed by this new wilderness, they would not expect anything from her or reproach her for her weakness. They were just waiting until it was safe to come back.

MARIE AND PARKER
THREW A PARTY

1.

The kids were happy, the adults were drunk. At 9pm, the Roman candles and sparklers lay on a card table outside the garage, right next to the cupcakes and deviled eggs. Junior Miller, underemployed contractor, stood near the table, gazing absently at his seven-year-old son dunking the skinny Harrington twins in the above-ground pool.

His wife Rina was singing karaoke under a rented tent in Marie and Parker Harrington's backyard. "Life is a Highway" was Rina's favorite song that year. Her earnest and off-key voice carried over the splashing swimmers. Over the rowdy group playing badminton with broken tennis rackets. Junior was on his third plate of barbequed chicken and coleslaw. When he looked up from his soggy paper plate, he saw a gray Jeep idling in the driveway.

The car remained running as Marie's sixteen-year-old daughter from her first marriage climbed out of the passenger side, cursing at the driver. The driver was a shadow to Junior, but definitely a boy, his head bowed over the steering wheel. The girl— for she was still just a girl to him then—wore crisp, white shorts and a blue halter, tied at the neck. He would always remember that, and how her long, blonde hair was pulled back into a ponytail.

Parker called Antonia "the bratty ballerina" because she took dance lessons and generally refused to speak to him. But watching her carry on a heated conversation at the open passenger window, Junior felt oddly protective. When she spun around and marched toward the house, he followed.

In the kitchen, Antonia began opening and slamming shut the laminated, white cabinets. Hideous cabinets, Junior thought, not for the first time since Parker had moved into Marie's termite-infested split-level a year before. If only he could gut the house, he believed he could work some magic. "If only," he heard Rina say, "you could get a real job."

"You're going to crack those cabinets off their hinges."

Antonia turned around, startled. "Junior?"

"I mean, there are worse things."

"This party, for instance." She jerked a thumb over her shoulder. "Check out the dude passed out under my dining room table."

Junior glanced into the next room. Rod Wilson was snoring on his back, t-shirt pulled up to his doughy chest.

"You okay, Tony?"

She narrowed her eyes at the nickname. "Sure, terrific."

It surprised him when she leaned into him and sobbed. The party was not the best he'd ever been to, but it wasn't the worst, either. Was she upset about the boy in the car? Teenage girls were a mystery to him. He put both arms around her. Her shoulders were hot and bony.

"It gets better," he said.

Antonia pulled away, made a face. Junior knew what she was thinking: what did he know about better?

Outside, the fireworks were starting. He didn't want her to go away upset.

"You want to light some sparklers? That might cheer you up."

She opened her mouth, and a shout came out of it. Had he made her uncomfortable? When her mouth closed and the shout escalated into a wail, he finally understood. Antonia wasn't making a sound.

He spun away, back outside.

A crowd had converged at the back of the garage, a spot hidden away from the rest of the party. He pushed through to Connor, lying on the grass and holding his hand to his ear, barely cupping the blood that poured from it. Rina had her arms around him, crying. Her wavy hair was damp with sweat. Her cheeks were still pink from the effort of singing.

The twins were crying, too. Their stepbrother, Jeremy, knelt beside them, his khaki shorts speckled with blood. He was speaking to them in his calm and grown-up voice: "Try to explain what happened."

He had the same hair as his older sister. The same critical, blue gaze.

"He wanted to show us how to light a firecracker," Darlene said.

Dara said, "We didn't think he could do it."

Rina saw Junior and yelled, "You were supposed to be watching him!"

Marie and Parker stood off to the side in their denim shorts and matching "Goose the Cook" aprons.

"Who keeps their firecrackers next to the snacks?" Junior said, but not too loudly. Parker had been good to him over the years—fixed his truck when it broke down, lent him money.

"We're calling an ambulance," Marie said. Her face looked the same as it always did: pleasant and untroubled.

Rina and Junior ended up driving their own car, Rina

holding onto Connor in the backseat, pressing her sweatshirt to his ear. She was a nursing assistant at the hospital, and she had already called a doctor she worked with, to let her know they were coming. After devoting her entire night to karaoke and Jello shots, she had still managed to take control of the situation, and Junior was the one who looked like the negligent parent.

It was his fault though, Rina was right. He needed to be more responsible. He would have to take better care of his family. That felt like the right thing to be thinking. But as he drove on dark and empty roads through Helena, watching out for deer, his thoughts turned easily from guilt to Antonia and how the top of her head had smelled like bonfire.

2.

The air felt crisp and promising. The music was easy listening. Marie and Parker's yard was dotted with lawn chairs, tiki lights, and picnic tables draped with German flags. No one in the Harrington household was of German descent, but Marie had found the flags on sale at Woolworths and decided they were as good a reason as any to throw a party. Everyone believed enough time had passed since the firecracker incident.

There were no hard feelings. People made mistakes, and Connor was fine. Better, perhaps, because even though he'd temporarily lost hearing in one ear, he'd learned an important lesson: not to light firecrackers without parental supervision. Tonight, Rina and Junior had hired a sitter.

Junior breathed in the smell of dry leaves and grilling burgers and smiled at Missy Richter, who was looking for a contractor to renovate her bathroom.

"Marie and Parker," she said, "they sure know how to party."

Thinking of the celebration Missy had missed that summer, Junior said, "You could say that."

Missy was looking good. Rina had mentioned it first, but

now that she'd said it Junior felt like he was allowed to notice, too. Her hair was darker and shorter than it had been in high school, and her eyes were bright and flirtatious. She'd moved away for a while, somewhere west, but now she was home for good and seemed to have a lot of money. Rina had also mentioned, "You're old pals. I bet she'd give you the job."

Now Rina was talking to her sister, Nancy, over by the pool, which was covered by a black plastic tarp and all the unused plastic cups. Although the night was cool, Rina wore a tank top, and she glanced over her bare shoulder at him and as if to say, *What's taking so long?*

Thing was, Junior wasn't sure how to turn a friendly conversation into a professional one. "Er, about that bathroom," he said, "I was thinking—"

"Come by on Monday, and I'll show you around."

He flushed. He wasn't sure they were talking about the same thing. "Okay." He caught Rina staring at him again and and gave her a tentative thumbs up. She raised her eyebrows.

Missy tapped her plastic cup against his beer bottle. "You always had a good eye, Junior."

He felt optimistic about his chances. First Missy's bathroom, then—"Thanks, Miss." One step at a time. He still had to come up with a reasonable amount to charge her. An old friend, yes, but a friend with money. He had to see how much work she really needed done. He excused himself to use the restroom.

Antonia and Jeremy sat with the twins on the back deck, playing cards, and he waved at them as he went inside. There was something sad about their little group, quiet in contrast to the lively party going on around them. Again, he felt that tug of protectiveness. Antonia looked older already, a serious look on her face as she zipped up Dara's hooded sweatshirt.

She did not appear to notice him.

Even in the bathroom, he could hear the music picking up tempo, the bass throbbing. Back outside, Parker stood behind the stereo equipment. "I'm taking requests," he said into a microphone.

"Always wanted to be a DJ." He laughed. "But then I grew up and had some bills to pay." A few people were already dancing, lifting their plastic cups as if they were lighters and this were a concert. Missy was trampling the grass with the rest of them, swaying her pretty hips. She winked at him and motioned for him to come out and join her. Junior shook his head; if there was one thing he didn't do, it was dance.

He rested gingerly on the arm of a deck chair. Jeremy was watching, making Junior feel like his body didn't fit where he was trying to put it.

"Don't you kids wanna join them out there?" Junior said. "Have a little fun?"

Antonia looked up from her cards. They were playing Go Fish. "Just what we're trying to avoid."

Dara said, "Antonia's dancing in *The Nutcracker* next month."

"Oh yeah?" Junior said. "I've heard of that."

"It's not what you think," Antonia said. "It's a joke—highlights from *The Nutcracker*, then little kids tap dancing to 'Jingle Bell Rock.'"

"We'll come see it," Junior said, suddenly enthusiastic. "I'm sure it'll be great."

Antonia looked surprised. "It's the dance academy's annual holiday recital. Only parents go."

He had more to say, more to ask. What had happened to the boyfriend? How was school? What grade was she in now? But here was Rina coming toward him, calling his name. She looked angry. Junior stood up. She tugged on his hand and came close enough that he could see the makeup gathered in the crevices around her eyes. Anyone watching from behind probably thought they were kissing.

Rina said, "Jesus, you're such a flirt."

It took him a second to realize she was talking about Missy, not Antonia.

"Calm down, Rina. I got the job."

"Well, she's out there acting like you gave her more than that."

It was almost midnight, past time to relieve the sitter. He looked back at Antonia, who was ushering the twins inside the house.

"Wait here a sec, I think I left something inside."

He made his way through the kitchen, through the dining room, up the carpeted stairs. He could hear the bath running, and then Antonia talking to the twins. Her voice was gentle and reassuring, and he headed toward it, though he wasn't sure what he'd say if he found her.

A door in front of him opened, and Jeremy stepped out. "Do you need something?" He only came up to Junior's chest. He was just a skinny teenager. But he had no problem looking Junior in the eye.

"No, I was just—"

"The kids are going to sleep now."

"—looking for a bathroom."

"There's one downstairs you can use."

"Thanks."

Outside, Rina waited for him behind the wheel. "I didn't think you were okay to drive."

His head felt leaden. Not swimmy and good the way it did when he was drunk. "You're probably right," he said. Slowly, they drove away from the party.

3.

Two hours till midnight, but people were already cheering. Some folks had gone inside. The smart ones, Junior thought. What a dumb idea it was, coming to another party with Rina. Coming here at all! Everyone forcing smiles and holiday cheer while they shivered in their coats and hats, drinking champagne out of fancy plastic glasses. His own cup was starting to melt from where he'd been holding it too close to the fire Parker had made in the middle of the yard.

"Happy Almost New Year!" Marie cried, lifting her champagne.

Her good nature irritated Junior. No one was that happy. She and Parker kissed, and not like they'd been married for almost two years.

In an effort to appear equally cheerful, Junior put his arm around Rina. "It's going to be a good year."

"I'm going home." She moved aside and pouted.

Now he didn't want to leave. "Party's just getting started, Ree."

"Well, you'll need to get a ride." They looked at each other for a beat before the flames lit up her sneer. "I'm sure Missy won't mind." She nodded her head toward the house, where Missy was standing on the deck, smoking a cigarette and laughing with Rod Wilson.

"Rina, give it a rest."

"Not until you do."

There was nothing going on with Missy, except that she was a difficult person to work for. Turned out, she wasn't looking for anything more than a contractor who could read her mind. She'd been disappointed with how the shower tiles looked, so he'd had to do the work all over again, for free. But he hadn't told Rina about it, since he was losing money on the job now.

Walking away from him, Rina's sneakers kept getting caught in the snow. Junior felt pleased to witness her small struggle. He felt his anger at her pressing at his chest from within, and that weight was not unpleasant. It felt like encouragement.

It seemed like a good time to have it out with Missy, blow off some steam. He waved at her, and she nodded her head in acknowledgement. But as he got closer, he could hear her murmuring encouragement in Rod's ear. The guy appeared to be crying, his thick shoulders bobbing under Missy's small, reassuring hand. The holidays, Jesus. Seemed like they were just created to get people down.

Junior walked into the house, as if he'd been intending to go there all along. He wasn't sure what he'd do next, or who he'd get a ride from. The house was full of people who shouldn't be on the road.

He moved past them and found Antonia pushing a mop

around outside the bathroom.

When she saw him, she grimaced. "Someone puked and someone else walked in it. Happy New Year to me!"

The words came to him easily: "You want to get out of here, Tony?"

She half-smiled. "I always want to get out of here."

They didn't talk about where; they just started walking. Out the front door and down the driveway, onto the quiet street.

There was no sidewalk in Helena, and they walked in the road, which shone with black ice. Antonia jogged ahead a little and blew into her bare hands, but Junior hung back, his feet unsure and slipping.

"We came to see your recital," he said, feeling awkward now that they were alone. He never went for walks in the neighborhood.

"I heard." Her head was uncovered, and in the bright moonlight, her hair looked white. "You went to all that trouble, and I was only in one number."

They were crossing over the bridge at the center of town, the one over Arbor Creek, now frozen over. Antonia paused and waited for him to catch up.

"You made a good snowflake," he said, sounding stupid to himself. "The best snowflake."

Stupid, but honest. He knew nothing about ballet, but even he had seen that her steps had more precision than the other snowflakes, who Junior thought were, quite frankly, mediocre at best. Their toes didn't stay pointed, they didn't always move in sync. He'd had to drag Connor there. Rina was reluctant but thought it might be nice to do something to "get in the holiday spirit." Even so, during the tap and jazz numbers, she laughed at the glittery costumes. "Dress them up like little whores," she whispered, while Connor kicked the seat in front of him.

A car passed them on the bridge, its high beams on. Antonia gripped the cold metal railing. Junior felt his anger at Rina nagging at him, goading him. He covered one of Antonia's hands with his own. "You'll freeze," he said.

She turned and kept walking.

Past Helena Mills, the large apartment building that once functioned as the actual mill on the creek. Past the old convenience store, burned down last year in a fire everyone in town assumed to have been started by the owner to collect on the insurance. On Main Street, they walked in silence until they reached the cemetery.

"What?" Antonia said, pushing open the gate. "It's the nicest place around. Always quiet, and everyone behaves the way they're supposed to."

"Because they're dead?" He felt a pleasant sense of bewilderment. She didn't answer. He'd never come to this cemetery before—never had any reason to. No one he knew was buried here. No one was ever buried here anymore. It was an old cemetery, and the gravestones were worn and white.

Antonia leaned against a tall one and ran her fingers along the inscription. "One of the founders of our thrilling little village."

He tried to read it, but there wasn't enough light, and the inscription had faded. Her face was close to his. He kissed her, very lightly. "It's probably midnight by now," he said. "Happy New Year."

"You're weird."

His heart was beating fast, but his head suddenly felt sharp and clear. "Weird looking?"

She shook her head and smiled. "Just old, I guess." She put her hand on the back of his head and pulled him to her mouth.

"Old," Junior said into her lips. But he'd never felt so young!

He pressed Antonia against the stone as her icy hands moved under his shirt.

Later, walking back home, the world had a new sheen to it. Junior didn't dare say it—he knew it sounded crazy—but it felt as if Antonia's talent had rubbed off on him. He thought he could do anything now—renovate a dozen bathrooms, make furniture for rich people, provide for his family, make Rina happy.

Antonia said, "I'm cold."

But when he reached out to caress her neck she moved away from him. The moon was behind a cloud now, and that unearthly light that had hovered over her had gone out. She put her arms around herself, visibly shivering.

He handed her his jacket, which she put on without looking at him.

"You okay, Tony?" That clear and shining feeling was shrinking from him, and in its place was a creeping dread. His life had seemed like little more than year after year of the same blank and shapeless thing. What a surprise then, to discover how little time it took for everything to change.

Passing over the bridge again, Antonia walked ahead of Junior, slowly, and she did not look back over her shoulder. He thought of Rina. When Rina was Antonia's age. What a happy girl she'd been in high school! What a beautiful girl, with big plans for the two of them. They would build a house, they would take their kids to Disney, they would buy a small boat to take out on the lake in the summers. She hadn't talked about those dreams in years. And that felt like his fault now, too.

Before they reached Antonia's driveway, they could hear the fireworks. They both stopped for a moment in the middle of the icy street, several feet between them, and looked above the tops of the trees. The fireworks were cheap ones that Parker had bought from a guy in a neighboring town, but they still managed to clear the trees, and Junior watched one bloom after another, sending down whispering, little sparks.

When the show ended, Antonia was already scrambling up a small hill to her front yard. Junior didn't move as she disappeared into the undergrowth.

4.

That year and a half at her father's had been terrible in many ways. Syracuse was ugly and gray, and she'd been practically friendless at the large high school while Jeremy blossomed into a social butterfly and extracurricular-king (orchestra, school newspaper, All-State soccer champion). And there was her stepmother, Jessica, always looking over her shoulder, checking on college applications and enforcing ridiculous curfews. But at least she'd found a decent dance school that had kept her busy until she graduated, and then she was on a plane in a flash, heading west forever, first to Oregon for a couple years of college and then Seattle, where she continued to live and work as a soloist in a small company. It was her fifth year in a row as the Sugar Plum Fairy in *The Nutcracker*. To tell the truth, the role had begun to bore her.

Thankfully, she had a little diversion: Jeremy was here for a visit. After several years wandering around the world, finding the best places to surf, and racking up quite an Internet following as a left-leaning political blogger. He was here with his boyfriend, Melvin, a tall and slim man who worked in advertising in New York.

Following the final performance of the season, Antonia took them to a party at a house near Greenlake, a party hosted by Lorenzo, a fellow dancer and on-again boyfriend, but it was kind of a grim scene: everyone was fretting about the state of the world (two wars they'd all protested, climate change) and what would they do once they were too old to dance. So Antonia escaped with Lorenzo and her guests to a little balcony off the master bedroom. Huddling in their wool hats, they gazed out toward the lake.

Antonia leaned against Lorenzo, feeling happy.

"Those kids," Jeremy said. "All the little mice, the party guests, the girl who plays Clara? How do they do that, get on stage every night?"

"Aren't they sweet?" Antonia said. "All of them, they're just really serious. All they want to do is dance! I see a lot of myself in them, actually."

She felt a sly little look pass between Jeremy and Lorenzo, who was behind her, but she could imagine his face: a knowing grin, *yeah, see what I mean?* And she ignored it, because this was her night. There were seven bouquets of roses in the trunk of her Volvo.

Tomorrow, Jeremy and Melvin were driving out to La Push, to surf.

"Your brother is crazy," Melvin said, smiling, proud. "In this weather? I'll probably just watch from the shore."

The way he was looking at her now, with sudden interest and admiration, he reminded her of Junior, how he'd looked at her that first time in her kitchen.

"You should come," Melvin said kindly.

Junior's face hadn't appeared to her in years, and now all those feelings flooded back. First, the pleasure and relief of being noticed. Then a wary sense of attraction, the fluttering excitement of walking in the dark with an older man. Of course, there was also the regret, which she had felt almost as soon as she had started to kiss Junior. In a graveyard—so morbid! Not to mention freezing. The whole time, he had clung to her more tightly than her first boyfriend the night they had lost their virginity to each other.

Jeremy smiled at Melvin, then Antonia, and his expression, too, brought back the years, how she had once relied on him. But she knew he would prefer to make the drive without her. She saw that little, warning flash in his eyes. Anyway, she had rehearsal the next day, a new ballet, choreographed by Lorenzo, that the two of them were dancing in together.

"Wish I could," she said, almost meaning it.

For a little while longer, they laughed and drank their wine while Melvin lit up a cigarette and did imitations of his boss, who spent the work day wandering aimlessly around the office, drinking Orange Crush and sharing his favorite lines from last night's TV shows as if he'd written them.

"He gave up his own dreams of being a screenwriter," Melvin said, "and now we pay."

Later, she dropped Jeremy and Melvin at her apartment, then headed back to Lorenzo's where she would spend the night.

The last time she saw Junior was the summer after her first year of college, when she was just starting to feel nostalgic. The twins were eager to spend time with her, and she'd driven them all over the county every day for a week, swimming in every body of water they could think of, staying out of the house as much as possible because—well—some things never changed. At Settler Falls, while waiting for the girls to change out of their swimsuits, she saw Junior walking across the parking lot, carrying a fleshy baby. She didn't know whose baby. He and Rina had divorced, but that's all she knew. Her mother and father wouldn't talk about Junior to her, because they thought it might upset her. They did not understand how much she'd wanted to talk about him—about everything. For her entire adolescence, it had seemed like everyone was afraid to ask for her opinion. And after news got out about her and Junior, Parker wouldn't talk to her at all. It was her fault, he said, that two good people had ended up so badly.

The Seattle streets were dark and shining now with rain. Antonia loved driving late at night, when there were few enough cars on the road that she felt like she was in a small town again and that the rest of her life was a big and wonderful thing just ahead of her.

When Antonia had seen Junior at the park, what had surprised her the most was how young he looked, how happy. His strides were light and confident. In her memory he'd been weathered and middle-aged, but incomplete like her. She wanted to call out to him, but the twins returned and wrapped their cold wet arms around her waist. "We're ready," they said. Antonia could hear Junior laughing with the baby.

DIATOMACEOUS EARTH

I tried to ignore Gerry's knock, but he wouldn't go away.

"You're in there, Catherine. I can see you."

I peered back at him through the kitchen window, the one that was painted shut: my unemployed landlord, grinning on the back porch. I couldn't see what had come over me the night before. I don't normally fall for men with conspicuous sideburns. But I opened the door, and he tried to kiss me. Outside, it was still raining.

"I brought down some beer," Gerry said. "I've got some steaks upstairs I could put on the grill."

Since he lost his job nine months before, he had been making his own beer. It was surprisingly excellent, but I don't think it saved him any money. He needed to buy a lot of equipment.

"I have all these papers to grade." I waved at the stack of student essays on the table. I'd been busily avoiding them with a gin and tonic and a crossword puzzle. "Raincheck?" I glanced meaningfully outside.

"For an English professor? You are very bad with puns." Inside Gerry started opening cabinets, grabbing glasses. "Anyway, isn't the semester over?"

It was, and after I reported the final grades, my job would be over, too. The department hadn't hired me back, although there was always the possibility I would get a call at the end of August, if they needed last-minute instructors. I didn't want to explain this to Gerry. As his tenant, I thought there might be a conflict of interest. Also, I didn't want to believe we were in the same boat, job-wise.

"These are their final projects," I said instead.

"Fucking hell," he grumbled.

Exactly, I thought, but he wasn't looking at the papers.

A stubby ant marched from Gerry's jug of hoppy beer toward the pile of dirty cereal bowls I'd been collecting for days on the counter. Gerry grabbed a sponge, and with as much violence as a person can muster with a sponge, pounded the countertop.

He held out the squished-ant side of the sponge for my inspection. "I think you have a problem."

"That's one ant. I wouldn't call it a problem."

Actually, I thought he might be right. Ants had been scampering across my dishes for the past week. And yet I'd done nothing. Dominic had been the one to deal with pests. I had no fear of rodents or bugs, but I never wanted to set the traps. Watching these ants move about my kitchen, I reasoned they had as much right to the place as I did. Their movements were deliberate and showed initiative: countertop, wall, a little exploration of the crumbs on the floor.

Gerry dropped the sponge and faced me, rubbing my shoulders.

"Don't be sad," he said. "Don't worry."

I could not tell what my face looked like to Gerry, which had been part of the appeal of sleeping with him: for those moments, I had stopped trying to figure myself out.

"You're probably right, Professor." Gerry grinned. "There's probably no ant problem."

With his soft belly and shiny forehead, with his perpetual air of unemployment, he should not have been so persuasive. But since Dominic had left that winter, I had missed sex more than I missed my ex-boyfriend.

Gerry pressed me against the counter, and I went along with it at first, along with his thin, eager lips. He was a good kisser, actually—generous, not desperate.

Then I became aware that we were no longer kissing and that Gerry was looking over my shoulder. "The problem, Catherine, is this kitchen is kind of a shithole." He eyed the piles of dishes, the crumbs on the counter, the jar of honey left uncapped. "These guys don't have to work for a meal."

I backed away. "You need to leave."

He started to protest, but I adopted the warning yet sympathetic look I'd perfected with the grade complainers—the ones who spent all semester skipping class, only to wonder where their very generous C- came from at the end of everything.

The next day I took the papers to my windowless office. Soon, it would no longer be my office, and I was trying hard to stay away, to let go of this tiny corner of my life that once felt much roomier with potential. But I couldn't risk being disturbed by Gerry, who had taken to painting the exterior of the house and making loud roof repairs during the days when it wasn't raining—"All the things I never had time for while I had a job." Back when Gerry was still commuting every day to Detroit, Dominic and I rarely saw him. We felt sorry for him—this divorced middle manager, forced to move into his rental property in Ann Arbor after his wife kicked him out of their much larger home in Royal Oak. She still got half the rent I paid Gerry, but he never complained. He told me he didn't want his kids to see their parents being assholes. Julie came around sometimes to drop off and pick up the kids, and we chatted when I was outside gardening or grading papers on the porch. She had a friendly, efficient manner. Her hair was always perfectly highlighted and straightened.

I had a bit of a shock when I saw my office mate had removed all signs of her existence overnight—gone were her posters of Globe Theater productions, all of her books with the encouraging titles: *Anyone Can Write!* and *Cultivating a Community in the Classroom*. All semester I had suffered through her endless parade of student visitors, the tender weepers and the enthusiastic gushers. Everyone loved her, and yet she had not been hired back either.

My office was on a long, dim corridor, silent now except for the buzzing overhead lights and the occasional chiming of the elevator at the end of the hall. The offices on either side of mine were empty, inhabited during the year by adjuncts like myself, a rotating bunch of writers and scholars who could not find tenure-track positions. When we gathered around the copy machine near the department head's office, we did not complain about job insecurity or low pay or our former colleagues who'd gone on unemployment the previous spring. Instead, we spoke about the inspiring breakthroughs of our students and the things we were learning about ourselves and our own writing. "Saps and martyrs," Dominic called us. "Consider the private sector," were some of his last words before he left teaching for Seattle and law school. But my fellow adjuncts and I believed in our stories in a deep, bodily way—at least in the early days. As the semesters and years went on, perhaps we went on telling them just to warm our hands by the fires of our earlier inspiration.

The air here was stale, almost odorless. I fanned the essays across my desk, turned on the computer, looked back at the papers—the accumulation of everything my students had learned from me. I had no Plan B.

I heard the elevator ding, then the flap, flap of sandaled feet walking down the hall. My heart caught—a student come to tell me how my class had changed her life? Or at least helped her write better papers for other college classes?

The fluffy head of Ava, the departmental secretary, bobbed at me from the doorway. She drank an iced coffee, the straw in her mouth, and held a bag of takeout, the corner of which dripped a reddish oil onto the carpet. Over the years, I'd made frequent trips to her desk to make idle conversation, but I rarely got my textbook requests in on time, and she never smiled at me the way she had at Dominic.

"Huh," she said, "You're still here?"

I looked around, as if I couldn't believe it either. "I was just leaving."

I turned off my computer and walked home.

It was lightly misting, but Gerry was still on some scaffolding, painting with small, halting strokes. How strange that he decided to become a landlord. Being a handyman did not come naturally to him. When he saw me coming up the sidewalk, I waved in a way that I hoped would be interpreted as distant and uninviting.

On the kitchen table, a few ants were having a little party with some crumbs on a week-old plate.

"That's it," I told them, "you're goners."

I took off my loafer and whacked the chummy crew to death, then tossed their bodies down the garbage disposal. With a new sense of purpose, I loaded dishes in the sink, filled the basin with soapy water, and while blasting public radio, washed those suckers like they'd never been washed before. After, I scrubbed the counters with hot water and bleach and vacuumed the floor. By the end I was sweating. I fell asleep on the couch with a box fan blasting directly on my face and slept straight through till morning.

I woke to the phone ringing.

"I'm sorry to do this to you, Catherine."

Slowly, I came back into myself, the living room, the fact that my life was kind of a mess. "What are you doing to me, Gerry?"

"I've got this—" He stopped, and then I heard his muffled voice, followed by other muffled voices. "Can I just come down to explain?"

"Give me ten minutes." I managed to brush my teeth and comb my hair. I wanted to look presentable, as much as I wanted to bolt the door against him.

Inside my kitchen, Gerry was overdressed in a dark suit and tie: suddenly a little handsome, his shoulders self-consciously back and away from his ears. He was breathing hard, and it occurred to me that someone had died. Julie perhaps. One of the children. I reached out for him, then thought better of it: maybe he needed to evict me. I was a few days late on the rent, as usual, and I did not know how long I had before he could tell me to leave.

"We're in for more thunderstorms," I said, sticking to the facts.

"Can you watch Ella and Stephen?"

I felt immediate relief. His eyes were a comforting hazel color, and I stared into them happily before realizing the kids were already on the back porch, squeezed into my papasan chair from Value Village and either tickling or torturing each other.

And there was the rain! It felt endless, biblical, stupid.

"I have an interview out in Dearborn," Gerry said. "This plant—they're hiring a Project Manager. Julie's at work, and it's some sort of professional development day at the kids' school..." He looked down at the floor. "I can take some money off the rent."

"Sure."

I said it because I thought I should, and then because I wanted to. Just the other night, we were sitting on the back porch and watching the thunderstorm, drinking the oak-aged bourbon his coworkers had presented as a thank you for his fifteen years with the company. "My parting shot," he'd called the bourbon, as we clinked glasses.

He opened the door and called to Ella and Stephen, ages eight and six, who surveyed the kitchen with critical, narrowed eyes—blue like their mother's. I was glad that I had scrubbed the counters so well. Not a crumb or an ant in sight.

"Hi guys!" I chirped, too perky for the demographic.

I realized it as soon as Gerry raised his eyebrows.

"Catherine here is a special lady," he said, blushing unattractively. "You know Catherine. An English professor at—"

"Well, not a full Prof—"

"Be nice to her. She has a lot of work to do."

Ella wrapped her yarn-thin arms around her father's waist, then nudged Stephen. "I hope you get it!" they cried as Gerry walked out the door.

Stephen whispered, "What if he doesn't get it?"

"He'll get it," Ella said. Then she turned to me, her expression hooded. "Do you have any good movies?"

"I don't even have a TV."

They stared.

Ella sighed, then patted Stephen's head. "We can watch *Magical Marsupials 3: Race Through the Outback* on my phone."

They slipped past me and onto the couch in the living room, where they curled up next to each other and gazed into this tiny screen, their shoulders hunched. I scooped up my stack of papers and took them into the kitchen where I barreled through them, relentlessly bestowing A's and B's to papers that otherwise would have been C's or barely passing. I didn't have it in me anymore to uphold high standards.

I was halfway through the stack when Ella strode into the kitchen. "Do you have anything to drink? If not, I can go upstairs. Dad always keeps pop around."

I thought of Gerry, what he would think of me once he saw me through the eyes of his children. Why did I care? I guess I didn't want to seem lame, even to him. "Oh, I have soda!" What I had was a vague memory of liters hanging out in the basement, waiting for a party.

Downstairs smelled like rotten eggs, even though Gerry had the dehumidifier going full blast. I stepped around a growing puddle to reach the shelf where I thought the soda might be: only generic cola, the label dusty.

Upstairs, Ella and Stephen were standing at the counter, gazing intently at a spot near the toaster.

Stephen looked up. "We killed these ants for you," he said, helpfully. The bodies lay flattened—black and crunchy—against the yellowed formica.

Ella shook her head and pointed at a tiny crack in the wall underneath the kitchen cabinets. "They were coming from there. It's, like, a colony or something."

"But I washed everything. There's nothing left to eat." My voice sounded weak and whiny.

Ella pulled her phone out of her pocket and started poking at it. When she held it out to me, I had to squint to see the Wikipedia page. "Ants don't like rain," she offered.

"Tell me how to get rid of them," I pleaded.

Ella frowned. Perhaps I was freaking her out with my gross, adult desperation, but she remained poised, if skeptical.

"Okay," she warned, "but I know a lot more about the plant life of Bali."

The kids followed me to the dining room, where my laptop balanced on a pile of newspapers. We crowded around it, and Ella told me what to search for.

"Google 'ant infestation,'" she said. "Or 'getting rid of ants.'"

She smiled at me, taking pity, and I had to blink not to cry. I had never felt so pitiable or in need of sympathy, especially not from a child. I thought of Ava, surprised to see me after I'd spent three years snacking on the Hershey's Kisses she kept at her desk, even though I hate milk chocolate.

"My mom says I am very resourceful," Ella said. I envied the pride in her voice, that lilt of optimism. Her fingers did a little dance on my shoulder. "In this economy, Catherine, you have got to be proactive."

After combing through online chat rooms devoted to households plagued by indoor ants, Ella, Stephen, and I finally settled on a remedy that sounded feasible and only mildly dangerous: diatomaceous earth, a powdery, porous substance that occurs naturally, is safe near food preparation, but illegal to sell in Ann

Arbor. I purchased a bottle online.

When it arrived, days after my afternoon with Ella and Stephen, Gerry was downstairs with me. He thought we should celebrate me being done with all my papers. Also, he felt hopeful about getting the job in Dearborn. "The interview went great. They responded well to my enthusiasm."

Gerry's enthusiasm. My secret, gloomy future. I guess that's why he and I had ended up in bed again, which is where we were when I heard the mail delivered. I put on a robe to go outside, and when I returned to the bedroom, I held out the package to Gerry. "I'm being proactive about my ant problem, see?"

Together, we laid the trail of diatomaceous earth: behind the toaster, leading from and to the hole Ella had spotted. "That's where they're coming from," I told Gerry. "They'll come out, gather the powder on their little bodies, and without realizing it, take it back with them to their nest."

"And then?"

I shuddered, in spite of my new conviction. "Eventually, they all dry out, become little husks of their former selves."

"Okay!" I liked his bright tone, so I kissed him, and he yanked open my robe. His hands were hot and straightforward. "Now we're getting somewhere."

I cleaned out my office on campus, brought my books and files home, and left them in the middle of the living room, with all the other mess. The ants had been gone for a few days. So had Gerry. I started to worry. And then I began seeing ants everywhere, littering the countertops and tables, before I would realize they were only crumbs or raisins—which I cleaned immediately, with a fervent energy. The surfaces of the kitchen always gleamed now, and I wanted Gerry to see them.

I told myself that I was making nothing into something. He didn't owe me a visit, the guy had real concerns: looking for work so he could pay child support and a mortgage. I just had myself to think of, and I needed to start doing it. I didn't need

Gerry's problems on top of my own.

I called the unemployment office in Ypsilanti to find out what I had to do, but you couldn't talk to a real person, and the line to the automated system was always busy, so I had to keep calling back. I kept hoping the busy signal would turn into a benevolent human voice, a fairy godmother with some job security up her sleeve.

While on the phone, I listened to Gerry's footsteps above me. It was strange I'd never been up to his place before. I hadn't asked to see it, and he hadn't invited me. Now, I desperately wanted to go. He seemed to be moving furniture. Vacuuming. Pacing. Talking on the phone. I wondered if any of the ants had migrated upstairs and whether he'd gotten the job. For three hours, he continued walking around while the busy signal echoed in my ear.

Five days without Gerry. I filled out the unemployment paperwork, applied to any open position in town. I checked my phone and email every five minutes for messages.

On a Saturday morning, Ella visited. When I opened the door for her, she barely said hi. "I've been doing more research." She looked pale and grim.

We sat at the kitchen table, drinking the generic cola from the basement, even though it had gone flat.

"I think you have carpenter ants. They're probably eating this house."

I smiled reassuringly, in spite of a new kind of anxiety plucking at the muscles of my throat. "I haven't seen an ant since we spread the diatomaceous earth."

Ella was not persuaded. She stood up and started looking behind things—the framed photos of the dog I grew up with, the one of me and Dominic I'd been unable to throw away: hiking in coastal Maine, genuinely happy. She peered into the crevice between the refrigerator and the wall, then walked into the dining room and through to the living area. "You have a lot of books," she said, passing them by, threading her way back into the kitchen, with me trailing behind. "There," she said, finally. "Under the windowsill."

And indeed, there was a single ant, making confused little circles. I got to him easily, pinched him with my bare fingers and let him fall into the garbage disposal. "I'll spread more powder."

Ella frowned. "There's always another colony around the corner."

The whole thing made my skin crawl. "Your father's going to be angry."

"We can't tell him." Her eyes filled, but she didn't look away. "He has too much on his mind."

I whispered, "The job in Dearborn?"

"He's afraid what you'll think of him."

This both touched my heart and set off warning bells. "I think he's great. Gerry's, like, wow, so great."

I reached my arm out to her, but I was too late to provide convincing comfort. Ella raised her eyebrows and headed toward the door.

"He really is," she said, before walking out.

While making coffee the next morning, I saw Ella and Stephen huddled once again in the chair on my back porch, and I went outside.

Their eyes were glassy. Stephen whimpered. "Our parents are fighting."

I could hear Julie's raised voice, though I could not make out any words. A moment later, she clomped down Gerry's rickety staircase in her platform sandals, stopping on the porch long enough to wave over Ella and Stephen.

"Hi, Catherine," she said, pleasantly. "I hope you're enjoying your long summer vacation. You lucky teacher you!"

I smiled and nodded, even though I was no longer a teacher, no longer lucky.

"Bye," Ella and Stephen said, a morose little chorus. Shoulders slumped, they followed Julie to the hunter-green Subaru in the driveway.

I didn't wait for an invitation. I walked upstairs and in through Gerry's open back door. The kitchen was immaculate, which didn't surprise me. The color scheme did, however: frosty-pink walls and canary-yellow cabinets—probably the whims of a previous tenant.

I found him in the tiny living room, where he kept his beer equipment stacked in the corner: white-plastic buckets and clear plastic tubes and tall, glass jugs. It had the clandestine feel of a grow room, the blinds heavy and drawn, the air moist, smelling of feet. The space was also, apparently, Gerry's bedroom when the kids were over. Once my eyes adjusted to the dark, I saw his immobile form on the pulled-out sofa. On the ceiling, dozens of half-peeled-off stars glowed faintly.

"My life's a mess, Catherine. You probably don't want to come any closer."

I sat next to him and took his hand. "My life's a mess, too." It was a relief to finally admit it to someone else. I kissed his forehead, then his lips.

"150 people applied for that one fucking job." He ran his finger along my collarbone, hooked it around the strap of my tank top.

"They fired me, too, Gerry. They're shrinking the department."

Snaking his arm across my lap, he grasped my hip, worked his way down my thigh.

We slid my shirt over my head.

"I could lose the house, Catherine. Julie wants to kill me."

Gently, I unzipped his jeans. "The ants are back."

I felt his eyes trained on me, seeing something I knew I wouldn't entirely recognize as myself. And in his gaze something flickered, a mad conviction that appealed to me. "Not for long," he said, pulling me closer. "We'll get them, you'll see."

We played Scrabble in the evenings, and I pretended that I was letting him beat me. The truth was, I'd never been good at Scrabble, but I wanted to keep up the illusion of my expertise. During the day, we skipped the job postings and surfed the internet for better ways to eliminate ants: trails of cinnamon, traps made with boric acid and maple syrup, an aerosol insecticide. We caulked up the hole behind the toaster and other gaps we found in the walls. Everything worked for a few days, but then we'd see a scout—a skittery, little lookout-ant—and we knew it was back to the drawing board.

And yet we fell into bed every night, almost euphoric. I showed him chapters from a novel I'd written in graduate school, and he declared me a genius. "I could be your agent, couldn't I?" he asked, undressing me. "I could help you get this published."

"Why not?" I declared. "We make a great team!"

I knew the novel was pretentious and dull, but I did not feel deluded as I encouraged him. When I looked at Gerry now, I saw potential. I saw how much he loved his children. Although the bank might own it soon, he started calling the house *our* house. We didn't divide his apartment from mine but wandered freely between floors. His ambitions were small but not meager. He made room for me and meant it. One afternoon as he heated water and dry malt on the stove to make his best beer yet—a delicate Belgian white ale that we drank in one evening—I asked him what he'd thought of Dominic. We'd never talked about him before, and I thought now how strange that was—that a reliable tenant could leave overnight and not be missed. His back stiffened then relaxed as he turned to me, his face sincere.

"I always thought you were too good for him." He smiled. "I thought you were this, I don't know, aristocrat. This *lady*. And Dominic was just your basic serf."

It was a thrilling and ridiculous thing to say. Hearing it made me love Gerry. I was sure I loved him enough.

And then the rain started to let up. It started to feel like summer, and then to *be* summer—clouds parting, grass growing too high in the yard.

Gerry refused to mow. He stopped trying to paint the house. Instead, he set up a couple of lawn chairs and a cooler filled with ice, and we spent the afternoons with a couple of cold ones, our feet in the weeds, reading the paper like people of leisure.

One morning while Gerry went out for coffee and the Sunday *Times*, I lay on his sofa and stared up at the peeling stars. For breakfast, I spread butter on a slice of bread and ate it with a glass of his American Lager.

And then I saw them—two ants dancing around the perimeter of the kitchen sink. I started for them, then grew tired of their insistent pace. Their inevitable return. I went downstairs, sensing a shift in my plans. There were no ants. But the furniture suddenly looked like Gerry's furniture, utilitarian and impersonal, even though Dominic and I had bought everything together, choosing each piece carefully from the secondhand stores around town.

On the day that I left, I took a long walk around the city. The tree-lined streets were pretty, but I was already looking at them like a visitor might. *How quaint*, I thought. *What a charming place to raise a family*. When I got back to the house, I walked inside through the front door, and from the long hallway, saw Gerry at the kitchen table, reading the paper. I felt overwhelmed by tenderness for him. He'd been a good landlord. He'd always called a plumber when I needed one; he tried fixing everything else, poorly but earnestly. He still called me Professor.

He looked up when he saw me coming down the hall, and his smile was so kind that I almost declared I would stay there forever. But then I looked at the wall where the counter and cabinets had been.

"What the hell, Gerry?"

"Amazing, isn't it?"

I wasn't sure what I was seeing: the drywall ripped out, the beams exposed. Gerry stood and handed me a glass of his latest—a light beer you could hardly taste.

We stepped over piles of sawdust, pieces of the wall. Outside, the cabinets were on the back porch, stacked haphazardly, hinges bent. On the kitchen table, I saw the red foreclosure notice pinned under Gerry's sweating glass of beer.

When I started to speak, he put his finger to his lips, reached for my hand, and pulled me closer. I felt the heat coming off him, but it wasn't an urgent desire. He kept just enough space between us. "It's their nest," he said, pointing. "Those used to be 2x6s." The wood was completely hollowed out and burrowed into. "They even ate the insulation."

The whole thing was oddly beautiful and delicate, like a formation in nature: airy like a wasp's nest, simpler than honeycomb. Or like sheets of weathered parchment paper, stacked sideways and burnt at the edges.

We stared at the layers for a long time, drinking our beers, neither of us speaking. The thing that surprised me most was that I couldn't see a single ant, much less an entire, functioning colony. No live ones, no dried up corpses.

"I have to go," I said finally. I knew that leaving would only solve one problem, the problem of staying in one place, and I was okay with that.

I left Gerry the furniture. He helped me gather the rest of my things into garbage bags and stuff them in the trunk of my '94 Corolla, which I'd had since college. Behind the wheel, I rolled down the window.

"Well, Professor..." Gerry trailed off.

I raised my hand for a high five. "We sure got 'em."

Gerry caught my hand in the air and kissed it. His shirt was still soaked from the effort of dismantling the kitchen.

On my way out of town, I stopped at Goodwill and gave away most of what I owned, which turned out to be less than I thought. I imagined that from Dominic's point of view, he hadn't left anything behind when he drove away; he'd gone toward something with a more definite, pleasing shape. The rain began again on the highway. I decided to head somewhere hot but dry. I wanted to be blinded by sunlight and blue skies. I wanted to start from the beginning. On the radio they were warning thunderstorms, hail, flash floods. Traffic was backed up on 23 in the other direction. In the slick black road, you could see the reflections of each car's headlights, burning like small but necessary fires.

ACKNOWLEDGEMENTS

My appreciation to the journals where these stories first appeared: "Faces at the Window" in *Hunger Mountain*; "When I Was Young and Swam to Cuba" in *The Saint Ann's Review* and *The SFWP Quarterly*; "Ph.D." in *Tampa Review*; "The Condominium" in *FiveChapters*; "Better Than Fine" in *Chicago Quarterly Review*; "Some of Us Can Leave" in *Carve Magazine*; "Say Something Nice About Me" in *Southern Indiana Review*; "Ports of Call" in *Sou'wester*; "Shelter" in *Southern Humanities Review*; "Diatomaceous Earth" in *Garo*, the online journal of the Rocky Mountain Land Library.

Many thanks to the University of Chicago Press for allowing me to excerpt Ben's poem "H [Hydrogen]" from his collection, *Particle and Wave*.

I'm thrilled the fantastic people of Augury Books found this collection and wanted to take it in. Thanks to Kate Angus, Kimberly Steele, Nicholas J. Amara, Julia Judge, Mike Miller, Isabella Giancarlo, and Ian Lloyd for their work in getting the book out into the world. Thanks also to my agent, Maria Massie, for guidance and encouragement.

I am enormously grateful to The University of Michigan, where a few of these stories began, and to my teachers there, whose influence continues to inform my work: Merla Wolk, Ryan Harty, Nicholas Delbanco, Khaled Mattawa, David Halperin, Eileen Pollack, Peter Ho Davies, and Michael Byers. Special thanks to Eileen, whose thoughtful instruction provided the scaffolding my writing needed; to Peter, for lending sanity and wisdom in all matters; and to Michael, for incomparable insights and for reading—and caring about—all these stories long after such a thing was no longer in his job description.

Thanks to the wonderful Ragdale Foundation, for time to be alone with my thoughts. And I owe a lot to the support of my cohort at the University of Michigan, the creative team at Enlighten, and my literary family in Ann Arbor. For their editorial insights, shout-outs to Lauren Pruneski, Emily McLaughlin, Bradford Kammin, Elizabeth Gramm, Kodi Scheer, Lisa Makman, Jane Martin, and Christa Vogelius. Thanks beyond thanks to Dana Kletter, the editor I always want looking over my shoulder. I am eternally grateful to Greg Schutz, for understanding what I was trying to do with these stories and helping me to do it better. And there are not enough *mercis* for my dear friend Brian Short, who read each of these stories with as much love as if they were his own.

Over the years that I wrote and revised this collection, I was fortunate to have the enthusiastic support of my family— amazingly creative people who have provided models for me of a life rich with the arts; thanks to my talented parents, stepparents, aunts, uncles, and cousins. I hope to provide that kind of example to my daughter, Iris, who has filled my life with the best reason for creating something out of nothing. Above all, thanks to Ben: first reader, wonderful poet, excellent baker, and companion in art and life.

Photo: Ben Landry

ABOUT THE AUTHOR

Sara Schaff's writing has appeared in *FiveChapters, Hobart, Southern Indiana Review, Carve Magazine, The Rumpus* and elsewhere. She graduated from Brown University, received her MFA from the University of Michigan, and has taught at Oberlin College, the University of Michigan, and in China, Colombia, and Northern Ireland, where she also studied storytelling.